MONTANA BRIDES

Welcome to Montana—a place of passion and adventure, where there is a charming little town with some big secrets…

Adam Benson: This ruthless corporate raider appeared to have it all. But what he wanted most was revenge—his enemy's daughter wearing his ring, living under his roof. And he had all the leverage he needed. If his bride declined, he'd destroy her family.

Victoria Rutherford: Her husband-by-force was no stranger. Years before, she'd found him attractive, though unsuitable, and ultimately a scandal of epic misperceptions had disgraced his family and sent them packing. Yet Victoria realised her husband's heart wasn't entirely encased in ice…and that he wasn't immune to his bride.

Crystal Cobbs: Her mystic aunt reported visions of the still-missing Christina Montgomery…and a crying baby. But some feel Crystal's the real seer…

Jordan Baxter: Loose-lipped Jordan continues to talk big about justice, but what kind of punishment does he plan for the powerful Kincaids?

The Marriage Bargain

VICTORIA PADE

*All the characters in this book have no existence outside the imagination
of the author, and have no relation whatsoever to anyone bearing the
same name or names. They are not even distantly inspired by any
individual known or unknown to the author, and all the incidents are
pure invention.*

*First published in Great Britain 2001.
Silhouette Books, Eton House, 18-24 Paradise Road,
Richmond, Surrey TW9 1SR*

© Harlequin Books S.A. 2000

*Special thanks and acknowledgement are given to Victoria Pade
for her contribution to the Montana Brides series.*

ISBN 0 373 65049 3

19-1101

*Printed and bound in Spain
by Litografia Rosés S.A., Barcelona*

VICTORIA PADE

is a best-selling author of both historical and contemporary romantic fiction, and mother of two energetic daughters, Cori and Erin. Although she enjoys her chosen career as a novelist, she occasionally laments that she has never travelled farther from her Colorado home than Disneyland, instead spending all her spare time plugging away at her computer. She takes breaks from writing by indulging in her favourite hobby—eating chocolate.

Victoria's next novel is due out next month. Look for *The Cowboy's Gift-Wrapped Bride*.

MONTANA BRIDES

Twelve rich tales of passion and adventure,
of secrets about to be told...

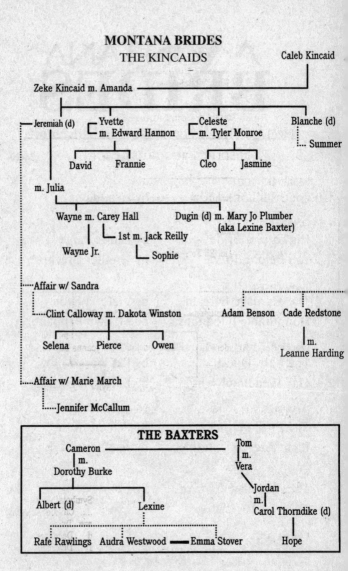

MONTANA BRIDES
THE KINCAIDS

Caleb Kincaid

Zeke Kincaid m. Amanda

Jeremiah (d)

Yvette
m. Edward Hannon

David   Frannie

Celeste
m. Tyler Monroe

Cleo   Jasmine

Blanche (d)

⋯ Summer

m. Julia

Wayne m. Carey Hall

Wayne Jr.

1st m. Jack Reilly

Sophie

Dugin (d) m. Mary Jo Plumber
(aka Lexine Baxter)

Affair w/ Sandra

Clint Calloway m. Dakota Winston

Selena   Pierce   Owen

Adam Benson   Cade Redstone

m.
Leanne Harding

Affair w/ Marie March

Jennifer McCallum

THE BAXTERS

Cameron
m.
Dorothy Burke

Tom
m.
Vera

Jordan
m.
Carol Thorndike (d)

Albert (d)   Lexine

Rafe Rawlings   Audra Westwood ━━ Emma Stover

Hope

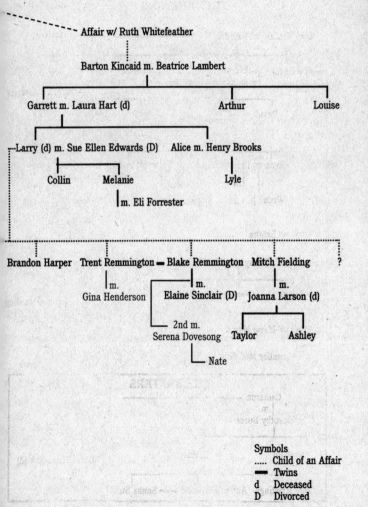

Affair w/ Ruth Whitefeather

Barton Kincaid m. Beatrice Lambert

Garrett m. Laura Hart (d)   Arthur   Louise

Larry (d) m. Sue Ellen Edwards (D)   Alice m. Henry Brooks

Collin   Melanie   Lyle

m. Eli Forrester

Brandon Harper   Trent Remmington ▬ Blake Remmington   Mitch Fielding   ?

m.   m.   m.
Gina Henderson   Elaine Sinclair (D)   Joanna Larson (d)

2nd m.   Taylor   Ashley
Serena Dovesong

Nate

Symbols
..... Child of an Affair
▬ Twins
d Deceased
D Divorced

One

Victoria Rutherford had fantasized about her wedding day since she was a little girl. She'd imagined that she'd wear a beautiful white off-the-shoulder gown with a wide, lacy skirt and a ten-foot train trailing behind her. She'd pictured her father walking her proudly down the aisle of a candlelit cathedral decorated with flowers and filled to the brim with friends and family. She'd dreamed of a groom waiting at the end of that aisle who watched her approach with a beaming smile on his handsome face, a groom who loved her so much she could feel it emanating from him.

Well, that might have been what she'd fantasized about, imagined, pictured and dreamed of, but it definitely wasn't how this wedding would be.

Her wedding.

That wasn't how her wedding would be in any way, shape or form.

Because there she was, standing in a public rest room across the hall from the judge's chambers where the ceremony would begin in ten minutes. And rather than a beautiful white off-the-shoulder gown, she was wearing just what she'd been dressed in when she'd arrived in her old hometown of Whitehorn, Montana, early that morning—navy-blue slacks and a lightweight pale blue sweater set.

There would be no gown. No cathedral full of well-wishers. No proud father to give her away.

And there certainly wouldn't be a beaming groom emoting a great love for her.

Never in her wildest fantasies, imaginings, picturings, or dreams had it occurred to her that part of the real estate deal she'd come to Whitehorn to take care of on behalf of her mother and terribly ill father would have involved getting married this afternoon.

The shock of it all showed on her face as she stared at herself in the rest room mirror. Her normally healthy peaches-and-cream skin was pale. Her usually lush lips were washed-out, too. Only her blue eyes and what she considered reasonably long eyelashes offered any color at all. Even her wavy blond hair seemed to have lost its life, falling to just below her shoulders much more limply than it had when she'd left her father's bedside in Denver at dawn.

"Some bride you'll make," she said to her reflection.

Then again, under the circumstances, what could she expect?

Who forced a person to marry him these days? she asked herself, still reeling from what had transpired since her arrival in Whitehorn.

She'd come back to the Montana town to do what ill health prevented her parents from doing—sign the papers that sold their once profitable but now failing ranch.

In its glory days the ranch had been home to her,

her mother Clarissa and her father Charles. A glorious home that had provided an income substantial enough to launch her father into several other business ventures and make him a wealthy man. One of the wealthiest in Whitehorn.

But then her dad had gotten sick with degenerative kidney disease and his medical expenses had begun to drain away everything.

Her father had always been in robust health and hadn't seen a reason to carry more than the bare minimum of medical insurance. He'd been sure that he would always be able to afford whatever the insurance didn't cover should he or his wife become ill.

But he'd underestimated just how expensive prolonged medical care could be.

In the three years since he'd gotten sick he'd had to sell off everything but the ranch to foot the bills. He'd held on to it even though he and Victoria's mother had had to move to Denver to be near the dialysis treatments that were keeping him alive.

But the ranch had been generating far fewer profits without her father running it and had, in fact, become a strain on her parents' already overburdened financial situation.

Victoria had helped out where she could, but a college philosophy teacher's salary—even at Boston University—was hardly enough to pick up the slack. And so, reluctantly, her parents had opted to sell the ranch.

Although Victoria hadn't been in on the decision, she didn't doubt that it had been a sad day when it was made. She knew how much her father loved that ranch. She knew that nothing short of desperate need would have brought him to that point, despite his denial that the need was all that desperate.

So the ranch had gone up for sale.

Within two weeks a buyer had made an offer. By proxy. None of them had realized how important the cloak of that proxy was.

Until today when Victoria had learned the truth.

Well, part of it, anyway.

She'd learned who was lurking behind that proxy and what were his terms for finalizing the sale, though not why he was setting those terms.

Adam Benson was the buyer.

"Adam Benson," she whispered to the mirror, as if she'd have more luck getting it to sink in if she said his name out loud.

There are people in every life who aren't forgotten. Who can't be forgotten, no matter how hard you try. For Victoria, Adam Benson was one of those.

Victoria remembered the son of her father's ranch hand and her mother's maid long ago. She remembered him and what she'd done to him, to his whole family.

She never thought of him without feeling ashamed of herself. And guilty. Very, very guilty.

She would have thought she was the last person on earth whom he would want anything to do with. And for good reason. Instead, he was making the sale of the ranch contingent upon one thing—her marrying him.

"It's crazy," she told her image in the mirror. Totally and completely crazy.

Maybe the man had gone insane since the last time she'd seen him when they were both teenagers.

But he hadn't seemed insane when she'd met with him that morning at his insistence. Cold. Calculating. Arrogant. But not insane.

She hadn't found it strange when the Realtor had said the buyer wanted a moment alone with her before signing the papers. She'd figured he might want to ask when the furniture would be removed or who among the ranch hands were worth keeping and who weren't. Something simple, innocent.

In her wildest dreams it had never occurred to her that she would find herself alone in a room with Adam Benson.

The years had been kind to him—that was the first thing that had struck her when she'd recognized him. He'd always been a good-looking guy and time had only improved upon that.

He was tall—Victoria judged him to be at least six-two—and had a muscular, athletic body in a suit that had to have cost four thousand dollars if it cost a penny. His shoulders were broad and straight, blocking her view of anything behind him. His waist was narrow, his hips lean, and his legs long and thick.

He was solid, substantial, imposing, commanding. He'd become a man who filled a room all by himself. Whose power infused it and left no doubt that he was calling the shots and would have it no other way.

Maturity had chiseled his features to sharply honed lines. His cheekbones were high and his entire jawbone was so defined and strong that she thought one tilt of his prominent chin was enough to make other men pause.

His lower lip was slightly fuller than his upper, but, oh, what a divinely sensuous curve that upper one had developed just below a nose that was finer than any surgeon could ever sculpt.

His hair was raven-black and he wore it short on the sides, barely long enough on top to comb back and all so impeccable she'd wondered if he had it cut every day.

As if all that wasn't enough, dark brows arched over penetrating gray eyes the color of pewter. Eyes that hadn't left her from the moment she'd walked into the room. Eyes that hadn't wavered. Or warmed.

He'd laid out his terms then, in what Victoria had learned right away was actually a business meeting. A business meeting in which he had the upper hand. A business meeting that began and ended with an ultimatum—marry him and the deal went through.

Reject him and it didn't.

If she rejected him, not only did she nix the deal with him, but he assured her that he would use his wealth, power and influence to block the sale of the ranch to anyone else.

At first Victoria had thought he was out of his mind and hadn't taken either his ultimatum or his threat seriously. How could he prevent the sale to anyone else? He had no hold over her or her family or the ranch.

"One phone call," he'd assured her mildly, confidently. "Do you think any bank anywhere in the world would turn down a deposit of a couple million from me if all I'm asking in return is that it deny a loan to any buyer of yours?''

Cold. Calculating. Arrogant.

And deadly serious.

Victoria didn't know what had happened to Adam Benson in the years since he and his family had left Whitehorn. But she did know he had cash for the million-and-a-half offer he'd made for the ranch. And from the looks of him, that million and a half was pocket change.

She didn't doubt he had the money to make good on his threat.

But marry him? Why would he want her to marry him?

She'd asked that point blank.

But he hadn't given her an answer. Instead one side of that sensuous mouth had raised in a slow smile that was more smug and satisfied than amused.

All he'd said was, ''Those are my terms. Marry me, we sign the marriage certificate first, then the papers for the sale. Or no deal.''

It just didn't make any sense.

She hadn't believed what she was hearing.

And yet there he'd been, standing right in front of her, dwarfing her five-foot-six-inch frame and laying out his ultimatum as if he were demanding nothing more than the inclusion of the refrigerator in the sale.

She'd never envisioned herself as a home appliance and so had not jumped to agree to what he was insisting.

Her hesitation had inspired the playing of more of his hand.

He'd pulled out her parents' financial statements—something she had no idea how he'd gotten hold of, something she'd never seen herself. They proved in black and white just how much her parents needed the deal to go through, more even than they'd let her know.

As if that wasn't enough, he'd upped the ante with projections of the future costs of keeping her father alive.

In short, Adam Benson had let her know that he had her just where he wanted her and wasn't above coming in for the kill.

And this was the man she was going to marry.

That thought sent a chill through her veins.

Because no matter how good-looking he was—and he *was* drop-dead gorgeous—he was alarmingly austere. The slight air of the bad boy that had been so alluring when they were teenagers had taken on a much harder edge. Now he seemed downright dangerous.

He *was* dangerous, she reminded herself. He was dangerous to her family's future.

Which meant one thing in Victoria's mind—she didn't have any choice but to marry Adam Benson. Whether she understood why he was pushing for it or not, whether she liked it or not.

''So buck up, because this is what you have to do,'' she told her reflection, noticing that her thoughts about this whole thing had washed even more color out of her face.

A knock on the rest room door made her jump and

realize once more how unnerved she was by what she was about to do.

"Miss Rutherford?" came a voice from outside the door, a man's voice that she recognized as that of Adam Benson's assistant. "Mr. Benson says it's time for the ceremony."

Victoria's heart felt as if it were in her throat.

Time for the ceremony...

He might as well have said, "The gallows are ready for your hanging..."

In her mind that was what this really seemed like. And she wasn't sure she could go through with it.

But then she thought about her parents, childhood sweethearts who still adored each other.

She thought about her dad, his indomitable spirit and positive outlook still shining through even debilitating illness.

She thought of that financial statement Adam had produced that proved just how much they needed the money.

And she thought about the fact that she alone could make it happen. That she alone could ensure that her parents had what they needed.

She took a deep breath and held it until her face turned red and her shoulders had floated up as if attached to balloons. Then she exhaled and made sure her shoulders stayed there—straight and strong and determined—a miniature version of Adam Benson's own shoulders.

"I can do this," she told herself. No matter why he wanted her to. "I can do this."

The assistant knocked and called her name again.

Victoria pushed herself away from the counter where her hands had been clutching the edge without her even realizing it. She marched to the door, opened it and held her chin high as she crossed the hall to the judge's chambers where Adam Benson waited for her.

Lethally handsome.

Cold as stone.

Somehow when she looked up at his face and took her place by his side, she couldn't help thinking that this was only the beginning of what he had planned for her....

"I now pronounce you man and wife. You may kiss the bride."

The wedding ceremony took fifteen minutes, start to finish. But when it was over Adam didn't kiss Victoria. He barely turned toward her, looked her up and down in a way that made her want to squirm, and said, "I'll bet you're sorry now that you didn't speak up."

And that was that.

The marriage certificate was signed. The real estate papers were signed. And his assistant, his lawyer, and the Realtor followed them out of the courthouse into the late-day October sunshine.

A few feeble and perfunctory congratulations were extended but Victoria didn't respond to them. In fact, she didn't say anything at all through the goodbyes to the Realtor and even through the limousine ride that placed her alone in the back seat with Adam while his assistant and attorney rode up front with his driver.

Instead, in the confines of the tinted windows, Victoria just kept thinking about the comment Adam had made at the end of the ceremony.

I'll bet you're sorry now that you didn't speak up...

So that was what this was all about. Revenge.

There wasn't time to ask him if it was true before the limousine pulled up in front of the main house on the Kincaid ranch, of all places, and put a whole lot of other questions in Victoria's mind as she was ushered out of the car and her single suitcase was unloaded from the trunk.

The Kincaid house was a sprawling home that Victoria knew well from her childhood days in Whitehorn. But then, no one in Whitehorn was unfamiliar with the Kincaid spread. In its heyday it had been something to see and even now, after having been vacant for years and recently spruced up, it was still an impressive place.

"Did you buy this, too?" Victoria heard herself ask Adam before she realized the words were going to come out.

He'd been speaking to his entourage and stopped midsentence to glance her way. "No, I didn't," he said disdainfully. "But since I'm a member of the family I have access to the house."

A member of the family? The Kincaid family? Adam Benson was a Kincaid?

That was news to Victoria and even more questions flooded her mind.

But this wasn't the time to ask them. She got that message loud and clear when Adam turned his back to her and went on with whatever it was he was saying to his assistant and attorney as his chauffeur disappeared inside the house with her suitcase.

When the chauffeur returned, the other two men assured Adam everything would be taken care of and said their goodbyes. Then they got into the rear of the limo and the chauffeur drove off, leaving Victoria and Adam standing alone.

Victoria's curiosity was too intense to be contained any longer than that.

"You're a Kincaid?" she asked.

Adam turned his handsome face toward her slowly, raising only one eyebrow at her. "Don't sound so surprised," he said facetiously. "Or do you figure I'm not good enough for that to be true?"

"I just didn't know," she said defensively.

"Neither did I. Until this past spring. I knew I was born out of wedlock, that my birth mother had gotten pregnant in high school during a post-football game fling with a player on the other team, and that she'd died giving birth. I knew my birth mother's sister was who raised me. But no one knew exactly who my father was—my birth father."

"And he was a Kincaid?"

"Larry Kincaid."

Victoria knew the stories about the Kincaids, even most of the stories about those who had passed away before her birth. No one grew up in Whitehorn without hearing them, despite the fact that there hadn't been any Kincaids in Whitehorn for a stretch. Unless she was mistaken, Larry Kincaid was one of the less savory members of the family, having been a womanizer, a gambler and a drinker.

"Larry Kincaid was your father?"

"Apparently. Although when my birth mother told him she was pregnant they were both too young and scared to do anything about it and he just hightailed it home rather than own up to what he'd done. By the time his conscience got a hold over him and he tried to contact her again she'd already delivered me alone and in secret, dying in the process. I'd been given to my birth mother's older sister and her husband to raise so Larry figured he'd leave well enough alone. That makes me the first of Larry Kincaid's illegitimate sons, a Kincaid myself," Adam explained.

"The *first* illegitimate son?"

"There are seven of us. It seems that Larry Kincaid had a few moments of regret about his escapades and during one of those moments he wrote down his amorous history and acknowledged the existence of his sons. He just sealed it away in an envelope in a safe-deposit box. After he died—of a heart attack in the middle of a bath while smoking and drinking—my grandfather found the envelope and decided to try doing right by his illegitimate grandsons. He arranged for us to meet here this spring to get to know each other. He means for this place to belong to us. If the deal goes through."

Victoria had left Whitehorn when she went to college and had been back only for occasional visits with her parents before they'd moved. Some news from Whitehorn her parents had kept her up on but not everything. Certainly not much of anything in the past three years since they'd left and conversations had revolved around her father's health. So she wasn't current on the goings-on in her old hometown.

"What deal needs to go through for this place to belong to you?"

"It's a long story," he said, clearly having no intention of telling it now. "You only need to know that I have every right to be here."

Oh, yeah, the man had a bone to pick with her, all right. His tone was as pointed as a saber.

"Not that we'll be here for more than tonight," he continued. "I own a small spread at the foot of the mountains that'll be more suited for our honeymoon."

He said that so derisively that he made it clear he didn't intend their honeymoon to be a great deal of fun.

But she opted for ignoring the entire subject and asking one more question about the Kincaid ranch. "If you own another ranch around here and you're probably going to own this place, why buy ours? It isn't half as big as this."

"As a matter of fact, yours is actually only a fraction the size of this one. This one is valued at ten million."

"So why bother with ours?"

His mouth stretched into a smile she didn't like. "Let's call it comeuppance."

Or just plain revenge, she thought, feeling as if he'd confirmed her earlier musings.

Another chill ran through Victoria but Adam didn't seem to notice. Instead he swept a big, powerful hand in the direction of the ranch house, motioning for her to precede him to the front door.

Every instinct in Victoria urged her to run the other way. To escape.

But she knew she couldn't do that. Her parents' future depended on her. She had no doubt that were she not to go through with whatever Adam Benson had in mind, he'd do everything he could to crush them all.

So she pulled her shoulders back, held her head high, and walked to the house with all the dignity she could muster, pretending she didn't hear the soft, satisfied chuckle that came from behind her as he followed.

Inside, the house was the same as she remembered it from years ago, except that now the furniture that had been so fashionable was dated. But still the place was large and comfortable and homey, although under the circumstances Victoria felt anything but at home.

If anyone else was there, they didn't come to greet them.

"Are we alone here?" she asked.

"For the moment. But we aren't the only ones staying here, no."

He didn't offer any more information, though. He merely stretched out a long arm, pointing to where she was to go, and he again followed her.

"You'll be in that room," he said when they'd reached one of the seven bedrooms.

Victoria turned into the well-appointed space where a big double bed made her mouth go dry.

Would they be sharing it? she couldn't help wondering with a tightening in the pit of her stomach.

But he'd said *she* would be in this room. Not *they*. So maybe there was hope....

"I'll have your dinner sent in to you. Don't stay up late. I want to make an early start of it tomorrow."

"Am I a prisoner here? Are you going to lock me in?" she asked. What he'd said and the way he'd said it caused her to think that might be so.

"The ranch hands and the hired help don't eat with the family, remember?"

"'The ranch hands and the hired help,'" she repeated, surprised and disheartened to be categorized either way. "Which am I?"

"Both," he answered succinctly.

But not family. Marriage didn't make her family.

"Fine," she said as if he hadn't stung her when, for some reason she didn't understand, he had.

Their eyes met then and locked together. His were as hard as steel.

What have I gotten myself into? she thought.

Despite the fact that she couldn't be sure just how far she should push things, she said, "So the tables have turned, is that what you're telling me? Now you're the family and I'm the help?"

"The tables have definitely turned," he assured her.

"And this marriage? What exactly will it entail?" she asked in a sudden burst of courage.

"Anything and everything I decide it will entail," he answered.

"Until death do us part?"

"Or until I'm satisfied."

"Satisfied?" *In what way?* she wanted to demand. But she couldn't bring herself to.

"Satisfied," he repeated in confirmation.

"And once you are? We'll divorce and I'll be free and you won't do anything to harm my parents."

"Are you asking me if that's the way it will be or telling me?"

There was a challenge in his voice that said she'd better not be telling him that was the way it would be.

"Is that the way it will be?" she reiterated.

"Maybe. If you're a good girl."

A good girl—the term and his condescending tone rankled. But she was certain it was meant to and refused to let it show.

"So this won't go on forever," she concluded instead.

"Forever? Literally? No, I don't think so. But it may seem like forever to you."

Victoria didn't say anything else. He was obviously enjoying this exchange and the power he had over her and she didn't want to feed into that any more than she already had.

Adam took his cue and said, "Be ready to go by seven-thirty tomorrow morning."

He spun on his heels then and walked out of the room.

Victoria watched him go, hating that she couldn't help but notice what a striking specimen of a man he was with those incredibly broad shoulders encased in the finest suit she'd ever seen.

When he was gone and she was alone in the room, she took another deep breath, sighing it out this time in relief at knowing they wouldn't be spending the night in the same bed, that he wouldn't be forcing himself on her.

But at the same time she also found herself wondering what it might have been like to meet up with him again under different circumstances, with neither of them carrying any kind of baggage from the past.

And she also found herself thinking that if that had happened, deep down inside her there might have been a hint of the attraction for the man that she'd secretly harbored so long ago for the boy.

Two

After a wedding night spent sleepless for the wrong reasons, Adam had some doubts about the wisdom of forcing Victoria to marry him.

Comeuppance. That was what he'd told her this was. That was his goal.

But as he showered the next morning, he had to wonder what was going on with him.

Leaving her alone in her room for dinner the night before was only the beginning of what he had planned for her. And it was appropriate. Certainly neither he nor his parents would ever have shared a meal with the Rutherfords.

So why had the thought of her all by herself with a tray of food in an isolated bedroom taken away his own appetite? Why had he been thinking about her at all?

He shouldn't have been. That was the point.

And now here he was feeling the damnedest twinge of something that seemed like eagerness to see her again. What was that all about?

He wanted to believe he was just champing at the bit to get this revenge under way. But if he was honest with himself he had to admit that wasn't all there was to it.

And if that wasn't all there was to it, then the plain and simple, clear-cut comeuppance he had in mind might be more complicated than he'd anticipated. Especially if he let himself feel anything that even bordered on attraction to Victoria Rutherford.

Attraction?

To Victoria Rutherford?

Well, what else could account for his being eager to see her?

But how could that be? After all the time that had passed, after all the murky water under the bridge, attraction to her was the last thing he'd thought he would feel.

Satisfaction, yes. For bringing about a well-deserved retribution.

But attraction?

No. Never.

He wouldn't have it, that's all there was to it.

Yet, even with his mind set against it, things kept eating at him, anyway.

Maybe there was something in the air in Whitehorn, he thought, disgusted with himself. Something that made him lose the control that served him so well everywhere else. Something that made him weak. That made him susceptible to Victoria Rutherford even as he was finally getting the chance he'd always wanted to give her back a little of her own medicine.

Because he sure as hell hadn't expected to set eyes on her and feel anything but the contempt she'd earned.

But then, maybe setting eyes on her again was part of the problem.

Why did she have to look so damned good?

Why did she have to have that perfectly proportioned, compact little body with those breasts that barely peeked out from beneath that sweater and reminded him of things he didn't want to remember?

Why did she have to have skin that looked like smooth, flawless velvet?

Why did she have to have that wavy blond hair that gleamed and glistened and danced around her shoulders in giddy delight, and made his hands itch to dive into it?

Why did she have to have those big blue eyes the color of a field of cornflowers?

Why did she have to have that small, perfect nose? Those small, perfect, shell-shaped ears? Those high cheekbones that left no one ever having to guess that she came from the best blue-blood stock?

And why did she have to have those same lips that dipped down in the center and up so intriguingly at the corners and still had the power to make him lose his mind with wanting to kiss her?

Damn her, anyway.

And damn himself, too, for forgetting just how beautiful she was.

And just how vulnerable to it all *he'd* always been.

Adam realized suddenly that he was scrubbing his chest so hard that his own skin was beginning to get raw.

He stopped and stepped under the shower spray to

rinse off, wishing the water could wash away the thoughts of Victoria along with the soapsuds.

He knew better than to let emotions enter the picture. Emotions clouded things. If he let himself have feelings every time he took over a company, every time he split it into parts and sold off the separate pieces, he never would have succeeded.

And that was what he needed to remember now: no emotions. Get in, do what he wanted to do, get out. It worked in takeovers, it would work in this, too.

After all, this wasn't a marriage like the one between his half brother Cade Redstone and Leanne Harding the month before, he reminded himself. Theirs had been a love match. This was something else entirely.

"This is comeuppance," he muttered, hearing just the right amount of venom in the word to let him know he wasn't losing sight of what she'd done, of the kind of person she was, of what she had coming to her.

It didn't make any difference what she looked like. It didn't make any difference that deep below the surface he might have some faint stirrings for her left over from before she'd burned him and his whole family all those years ago.

He could control it. He could keep it under wraps.

He damn sure wouldn't let it interfere with what he had planned for her.

In the end, the reward in delivering his retribution would be so much better than anything that might come of some residual, misguided attraction.

And if he put a little speed into finishing with his morning routine because he was anxious to get things under way, it had nothing to do with her hair or eyes or skin or the breasts he'd actually dreamed about when he had finally fallen asleep the night before.

It only had to do with impatience to gain the reparations he was due.

It didn't have anything whatsoever to do with wanting to spring her from her makeshift exile or anything to do with wanting to see her again.

He was sure of it.

He'd *make* sure of it.

If it was the last thing he ever did.

"Crystal? Are you all right?"

The sound of her aunt's voice barely penetrated Crystal Cobbs's thoughts. She yanked herself out of her reverie and turned to find Winona standing across the desk in the rear of the Stop-n-Swap she helped her aunt run.

"I heard you scream back here," Winona Cobbs said. She looked closely at her niece. "You look as if you've seen a ghost. What's happened?"

"N-nothing. Really, Aunt Winona, it's…it's nothing."

"You've had a vision, haven't you?" Winona guessed.

Crystal nodded her confirmation. She knew her aunt would understand. The visions Crystal had were similar to those Winona herself experienced. Even though Crystal didn't want anyone else to know she had them, too, it was good to be able to confide in her aunt.

"It just happened. I saw Christina Montgomery…out in the woods, of all places." She stopped and took in a breath. "Aunt Winona, she was dying."

"Christina?" Winona asked. "Out in the woods? Somewhere you were familiar with? Or could point out to the sheriff?"

Crystal shook her head. "It was just the woods. In the mountains, I think."

"You should tell Sheriff Rawlings or Deputy Ravencrest," Winona advised. "That girl has been missing for too long and the sheriff's department doesn't seem to be getting any closer to finding her now than when she disappeared."

Crystal realized that was true but balked at the idea of revealing just how much like her aunt she really was by telling the sheriff or his deputy about her vision. She knew what happened when people found out about things like visions. She knew from seeing what had happened to her aunt. Winona was an oddity in Whitehorn. An outcast. And that wasn't something Crystal wanted for herself now that she'd opted to stay in the small town. She had only intended to visit her aunt after Winona's heart attack this past summer. But there was something about Whitehorn that had made her say goodbye to her Georgia home.

"It was so vague," she hedged. "I don't know what good it would do."

"You never know. But telling could send Rafe Rawlings and Sloan Ravencrest looking in the right direction or give them some clue as to what's going on with the mayor's daughter. It could lead them to find her.''

Crystal considered that. She was torn. She knew only too well that all of Whitehorn was abuzz over the mayor's youngest daughter. There had been some speculation around town that her less than pristine reputation as a flirt—and worse—had caught up with her and that she'd gotten pregnant by one of the many men she'd been seen with. But before anyone had confirmed that, she'd disappeared. Everyone was worried about her and the sheriff's department was conducting an all-out search for her.

If Crystal's vision could help, how could she not let the sheriff know?

But if she told him about it, her whole life could change. And not for the better.

If only she truly believed her vision would make a difference….

"What if I go to the sheriff and claim that I had the vision?" Winona offered in the midst of Crystal's struggle with herself.

That lifted Crystal's spirits. "Would you do that?"

Her aunt shrugged. "Folks around here already think I'm a kook. What difference does it make if they have one more piece of evidence to support it?"

"Are you sure?"

"Just give me all the details, no matter how insignificant they seem, and I'll relay them to Rafe and Sloan. If it helps, fine. If it doesn't, well, at least we didn't withhold information that might have been useful.''

Crystal breathed a sigh of relief. "I'd feel so much better if the sheriff knew," she said. "Think about the guilt I'd have to live with if my vision had some bearing and I didn't let anyone in on it."

"But you don't want anybody thinking you might be as weird as I am," Winona said with a laugh and without taking any offense. "I don't blame you. It isn't easy to have people think you're off the beam. Now fill me in."

Crystal did just that, although it didn't take long because there weren't any particular landmarks to distinguish what she'd seen.

About the time she was finishing, their first two customers of the day arrived.

"Why don't you go take care of them? It'll help get your mind off your vision," Winona said. "And don't worry. As soon as I can, I'll go see the sheriff."

"It's a deal."

Winona had barely turned to go before Crystal said, "Aunt Winona?"

Winona stopped short and glanced over her shoulder at her niece with a quizzical lift to her eyebrows.

"Thank you," Crystal said.

Winona just waved away her niece's thanks with both hands fluttering like bird's wings and left.

"How's Daddy?"

The first thing Victoria did when she woke up was call her mother in Denver and apologize for not telephoning the night before.

But Victoria had needed to think about what she was going to say to her parents. About whether or not she was going to tell them what had gone on the previous day.

"He had a bad night," her mother told her in response to the question about her father. "He's sleeping now but he was up until almost five this morning. Did everything go all right with the closing of the ranch?" Unfortunately a bad night was nothing unusual for her father since his health had deteriorated and so her mother didn't dwell on it.

"The closing was fine."

"Did you meet the buyer?"

"Yes." Victoria didn't offer more than that.

"Was it a family?"

"No. Just a single man."

Victoria had her fingers crossed that her mother wouldn't delve any deeper than that.

Apparently it worked because after a moment her mother said, "And now you'll be packing up what we left behind so he can move in?"

"Right," Victoria confirmed. Her mother knew she'd taken a semester's leave of absence from the University to do just that and the decision she'd come to during the night was to leave it at that. Adam had said this marriage wasn't a forever thing, that when he was *satisfied* it would end, so why burden her parents with the turn the sale of the ranch had taken? It would only upset them and what Victoria hoped was that Adam's *satisfaction* would come before too long, this sham of a marriage would be dissolved and she really could get down to packing up the ranch without her folks ever knowing what she'd had to do to accomplish it all.

"I'm worried about your taking time off work," her mother said then.

"You have enough to worry about, don't give that another thought. I told you it's all taken care of." Which was the truth and a lucky thing since she wouldn't have been able to return to Boston after all.

There was a click on the other end of the line just then and her mother said, "Oh, that's another call. Do you want to hang on while I see who it is?"

"No, why don't we go ahead and say goodbye. I'll talk to you again in a day or so. I love you. And Daddy, too."

"We love you, too. Don't work too hard. You have plenty of time to do all that packing."

They said their goodbyes and Victoria hung up.

But it wasn't packing what remained at her old family home that was on her mind when she did.

Instead she was hoping that she was right and this so-called marriage would be over before too long so she really could make good on her word.

"The Stop-n-Swap is where we're getting the clothes I'll need at your ranch?" Victoria whispered in disbelief as Adam led her into the junk shop on the outskirts of town. She didn't want the woman behind the counter to overhear her and be insulted, but she just had to make sure she wasn't mistaken. Even though the Stop-n-Swap carried some used clothing, it wasn't a place she'd ever shopped before.

"Not everyone has a personal shopper at a designer store," Adam seemed to enjoy answering.

"Now you get to see what it's like to dress the way I had to when I was a kid."

"I didn't know you had to wear used clothes as a kid."

"The Stop-n-Swap and the church thrift shop—that's where nearly everything I ever wore came from."

"And you blame me for that, too?"

He shrugged the broad shoulders that her eyes had been caressing since he'd knocked on her door an hour before and unceremoniously told her to get her rear in gear. "I just want you to know what it was like on the other side of the tracks."

"May I help you?" The woman came out from behind the counter and approached them.

Victoria might not have frequented the Stop-n-Swap when she'd lived in Whitehorn before, but she knew it well enough to know it was owned by Winona Cobbs and that this much younger woman was not Winona.

"We'll be needing some jeans, shirts, sweaters and boots, Crystal. For the lady," Adam answered with a negligent nod toward Victoria.

He didn't appear to have any intention of introducing them, so Victoria said, "Hi. I'm Victoria Rutherford…well, Victoria Benson now, I guess. Anyway, I used to live around here a long time ago but you don't look familiar to me. Did you take over for Winona?"

"I'm Crystal Cobbs, Winona's niece. I work with her most of the time, but she had an errand to run."

"So you're new to Whitehorn?"

"I've only been here since the summer. What about you? Are you back for a visit?"

"I thought I was just coming to take care of some business. But there was a...change of plans."

Victoria's involuntary glance in Adam's direction drew the other woman's attention. It was to Adam that Crystal said, "I didn't know you had a wife."

"Only since yesterday," he answered, clearly not meaning to expound on that, either.

"So you're newlyweds," Crystal said in a lazy drawl, as if that amused her for some reason. "Well, congratulations. I think," she added with a little laugh.

Victoria wasn't sure if it was the other woman's warm smile or just the pure relief of meeting up with someone who didn't treat her as though she had the plague, but Victoria felt an almost-instant connection with Crystal Cobbs. So much so that she decided to ignore Adam in favor of a little camaraderie with the other woman to help ease this unusual shopping trip.

"I'm apparently going to have a rustic honeymoon," Victoria confided as if she weren't as uneasy about it as she actually was. "Can you help me with a few things?"

"Probably not with what you really need help with," Crystal said with another glance cast at Adam. "But I'd be happy to help you find some of the clothes you need."

Victoria didn't understand, but Crystal looked from her to Adam and back again and seemed on the verge of full-blown laughter, as if she knew what was going on between them.

She contained her delight, though, and linked her elbow with Victoria's in a way that two old friends might join forces against a bully who was more bluster than anything.

"Come on," she said. "I'll show you what we have."

Victoria spent the remainder of the morning in town, following Adam as he ordered supplies to take with them to his ranch. The frugality he'd exhibited in regard to her purchases was nowhere in sight when it came to ordering pig chow, chicken feed, oats for horses, roof shingles, nails and various other hardware items, as well as a full stock of groceries.

Some of the stores weren't ordinarily open on Sunday but Adam had apparently arranged for special concessions and everywhere they went he was catered to as if he'd gained some kind of celebrity status.

While the big black truck Adam was driving in lieu of the limo from the day before was loaded with his purchases, he pointed at the Hip Hop Café and said, "We'll get some lunch and then head out."

The Hip Hop Café had been the meeting place in Whitehorn for as long as Victoria could remember. It was a dinerlike establishment with old-fashioned ceiling fans instead of air-conditioning, chrome counters that dated back to the fifties, a jukebox that could really get the joint jumping, and generally good, if not fancy, food.

Even at one o'clock on a Sunday afternoon nearly all the tables and counter space were occupied, but

Adam motioned for Victoria to precede him to a corner table in the back that had just been cleared off.

Victoria's appearance in the restaurant caused quite a stir. Since arriving in town the morning before, when she'd gone straight to the real estate office, she hadn't seen many of the folks she'd known growing up in Whitehorn. But a fair share of the people eating all around her wore familiar faces.

It was suddenly like old home week with folks coming over to the table or just chatting from their seats, asking how her parents were, wishing her father the best, letting her know the family was missed around town.

But more than her own reception, Victoria was interested in Adam's. Or actually in the way he responded to the warm hellos and how-are-yous that greeted him.

He was nice. Open. Friendly. Charming. Funny.

He didn't dish out any of the icy treatment he continued to serve up to Victoria. Instead he was as pleasant as she remembered him being as a teenager.

Even though she wasn't the recipient of any of it, Victoria took heart. Maybe the younger Adam Benson was lurking somewhere beneath the surface, after all.

But Victoria realized she wasn't the only person to bring out the icy side of Adam when Jordan Baxter walked into the café.

Jordan Baxter was not only someone she'd known from around town when she'd lived in Whitehorn as a child. He was also someone her parents had talked about since she'd left. He was not particularly well liked but he was well known as a poor boy who grew to be a success.

He was also known for his long-standing feud with the Kincaids and the moment he spotted Adam at the corner table, he made his way to it, ignoring everyone else in the Hip Hop.

"Well, well, well. If it isn't one of the new Kincaids," he said as he drew near.

"Baxter," Adam said in greeting, his tone and stony expression something Victoria had begun to think he reserved for her alone.

"I've been wondering when we'd get to meet again," Jordan continued, seemingly undisturbed by Adam's frigid welcome. "I have to say that ever since I found out who your real daddy was I've been torn about you, of all the Kincaid bastards. Over the years I've followed your rise through the ranks of the businessworld, you know. Admired and respected you. Thought we were two of a kind, you and I— both from Whitehorn, both from hard-scrabble upbringings, both sloughing off the stink of poverty, scrambling and working hard to get where we are. Imagine my disappointment at finding out you're a *Kincaid.*" He nearly spat the name. "A *Kincaid,*" he repeated as if he hadn't put quite enough hatred into it the first time.

"That's right, I'm a Kincaid," Adam confirmed, sounding proud of it.

Jordan nodded his head, never taking his eyes off Adam, as if Adam were an adversary worth watching. "Well, you may like your new family ties but don't think they're actually going to get you anything. Especially not that ranch you all wallowed in for months. That prime piece of property is rightfully mine and I'm going to see to it that that's how it ends up. Come hell or high water.''

"I've heard you're giving it a try, anyway," was all Adam answered, obviously unintimidated.

"Oh, I'm giving it more than just a try. You may be used to winning out against weaker foes, but I'm not one of them. Make no mistake about it—that ranch is mine.''

Adam merely shrugged one shoulder.

"But no hard feelings," Baxter added. "In fact, once I'm set up at the ranch, you and I might even be able to do a little business.''

"I don't think so.''

"Are you telling me you don't always need investors for your little coups?''

"I'm telling you you'll never be one of those investors.''

The bill for lunch had been set on the table just before Jordan Baxter arrived and now Adam picked it up as if the other man weren't still standing there. He glanced at the total, tossed a twenty-dollar bill on the table and stood. Then he pulled Victoria's chair out to let her know they were leaving.

Victoria wasn't exactly sure what to do. She'd never been rude enough to just get up and walk away from someone, without so much as an I-have-to-be-going.

But Jordan Baxter hadn't even glanced at her or acknowledged her in any way, so she wasn't the likeliest candidate for bidding him goodbye. And Adam was making it clear he wasn't staying for more of this goading chitchat.

She finally opted for muttering an, "Excuse me," as she maneuvered around Jordan to get away from the table and follow Adam toward the door.

"I'll have the last laugh on the lot of you," Jordan said in a loud voice to their backs as they left the café. "That ranch will never belong to you and your bastard half brothers. Count on it."

But he might have been shouting at a brick wall for all the response he got from Adam.

Adam had instructed that the truck be loaded and left out front of the Hip Hop with the keys in the ignition, and that was where they found it once they were outside. Without saying a word to Victoria, Adam got in behind the wheel.

It flashed through Victoria's mind, as it had just before the wedding the day before, to just walk away rather than to willingly get in the passenger side of that vehicle and go with him.

But, again, she remembered her parents and knew she had no choice, so she climbed into the truck.

Adam had started the engine and pulled away from the curb before she got her seat belt on.

They were headed out of town when she gathered the courage to say, "So what was all that about with Jordan Baxter?"

Adam let so much time elapse in silence that she'd just about given up hope of an answer when he finally said, "You know Baxter hates the Kincaids, that he has a grudge against them for the affair Jeremiah Kincaid had with his mother when he was a boy.''

"He thinks Jeremiah Kincaid set the fire in her apartment that killed her," Victoria confirmed.

"Right. And it's always stuck in his craw that just before his uncle Cameron died—when Cameron needed money—he sold off the old Baxter place to Jeremiah Kincaid, of all people. At the time he swore his uncle had given him the first right of refusal in the event of any sale, but he couldn't prove it, so the deal with Jeremiah went through and the old Baxter place became part of the overall Kincaid ranch.''

"I remember hearing about that.''

"When Jeremiah died, the property passed into trust for his illegitimate baby daughter, Jennifer McCallum, which is the way it's been until now. But just recently it was decided that the place should be sold and—like I told you before—when my grandfather heard about it he decided he wanted to buy it as a legacy for my half brothers and me. He wants it to be a home base where any of us can live or work or just visit when we want. Some place we can all own jointly to have the kind of unity we didn't have growing up, scattered to the wind the way we were. It's his way of bringing us all together as a family now.''

"That's awfully nice of him.''

"He's a nice man," Adam said simply. "Anyway, the sale was just about to go through, so we all met there this spring and moved in—to get to know each other. But about the time we did, Baxter says he received a letter from his uncle's lawyer, George

Sawyer. Seems that after Sawyer's death, as his family went through all his papers, they found the document giving Baxter that first right of refusal, after all. They sent it along to Jordan and he filed suit, claiming that first right of refusal on his uncle's spread gave him first right of refusal on the whole Kincaid ranch because they're one and the same now. He has the whole thing tied up in court.''

"Have you had dealings with him before this?"

Adam cast her a glance that said he couldn't believe she'd asked such a thing. "No. Why would I have?"

"From the way he talked at the Hip Hop, I assumed the two of you had crossed paths along the line."

"Yeah, we've crossed paths along the line. I met up with him at a business conference in New York a few years ago, before either of us knew I was a Kincaid. But even then I didn't like him, and I don't like him now. He keeps harping on that bit about all the two of us have in common."

Adam's tone made it clear he didn't agree and didn't appreciate the comparison. So much so that he didn't even seem to want to talk about it anymore because he reached out and turned on the radio, suddenly filling the truck cab with loud country music from Whitehorn's own radio station as they headed into the countryside.

Victoria got the hint and didn't attempt more conversation. Not that she could even if she'd wanted to over the loud radio.

Being alone with him in the enclosed space, without distraction, wasn't easy for her. It made her too aware of him, of every detail about him, every nuance.

Such as the way his hands rested on the steering wheel, mastering it with a steady, sure, relaxed grip. Big, hard hands that still looked as if he could put in a long day of ranch work without gloves. Hands that hadn't been softened by his current, less manual life-style.

His wrists were powerful-looking and lightly covered with hair as dark as that on his head, running up forceful, sinewy forearms before disappearing into the rolled-up sleeves of a denim work shirt.

She couldn't help noticing his thighs, too. Massive, muscular thighs encased in worn blue jeans, spread against the seat and making her remember the way they'd looked straddling a horse years ago. Making her flash on an uninvited image of those thighs straddling other things....

Her.

Victoria didn't know where that had come from, but she yanked her eyes up and away from him, yanked her thoughts from anything so ridiculous. She tried to calm the unwanted fluttering in the pit of her stomach.

But once the fluttering got started it was difficult to quiet. Especially when she found her gaze rolling to those broad shoulders and a chest that stretched the denim fabric taut, up a thick column of neck to that jawline that was sharp enough to slice bread.

Even clean-shaven he had a faint shadow of a beard. Darker, coarser, than it was when he was a teenager. She remembered the feel of it then—just a little scratchy against her face—and knew that now it would be more harsh to the touch. If they ever got that close. Which, of course, she hoped they didn't.

It was an incredible profile, though. Chiseled and fine, angular and perfect, beneath the raven-black hair that covered a head so well-shaped he could have been bald and would still have been striking. She couldn't help even admiring the shape of his ears and the way they eased into the side of his face on lobes that were somehow so sexy she could imagine herself taking a little nibble of them.

He caught her staring at him then and turned that handsome head to look her straight in the eye with those piercing, steely gray ones of his.

"Do you have a problem?" he asked.

Only as far as those stomach flutters were concerned. And they were going wild by then.

"No," she answered, pulling her glance away and forcing herself to look out the side window at the gently rolling land they were passing through.

But even without staring at him she was still so intensely aware of him that she couldn't get him out of her mind.

And she couldn't stop those flutters, either.

Which caused her some serious concern.

This was a man who had forced her to marry him, she reminded herself. *Forced* her. A man who had only contempt for her. She didn't want to have these kinds of thoughts about him. She certainly didn't want to have the flutters in her stomach that the thoughts brought with them.

And she wouldn't, she vowed. She just plain wouldn't allow herself to be so acutely aware of him. To think about him in anything more than a passing, incidental way.

That's all there was to it.

But as the smell of citrus after-shave swirled around her and the pure sense of his masculinity filled the truck cab so completely that she was enveloped in it, she wasn't too sure how she was going to go about keeping that vow.

She didn't doubt that she could resist him on the surface.

But keeping him out of her thoughts, keeping herself from noticing things about him that seemed to have a way of seeping into her consciousness all on their own?

That was something else again.

It took about an hour to get to Adam's ranch. It sat at the foot of the Crazy Mountains, just off the same road that led to the Laughing Horse Reservation a few miles farther into the hills.

The house came into view within minutes of turning from the main road onto the rutted one that led to it. It was a small log cabin with a covered front porch and a steep roof with one dormer window jutting out of its center.

An old-fashioned red barn dwarfed the house from behind. There was a small lake to the right with a huge elm tree whose branches arched over it to drop golden autumn leaves into the pool, and open fields stretched from there as far as Victoria could see.

It looked like a cozy place but it was definitely smaller and more rustic than she'd expected.

An old, dilapidated, rusted-out red truck loaded with saddles and suitcases was parked in front of the house. Other than that, there were no signs of anyone else anywhere around.

The sound of their approach brought a bow-legged man Victoria guessed to be about sixty out onto the porch. He leaned a brawny shoulder against one of the gnarled wood posts that stretched from the cross-buck railing to the overhang. That was where the man stayed as Adam pulled up beside the other truck. He only pushed off the post and came down the three steps when Adam got out.

"Hey, Sherm." Adam greeted him with the same kind of friendliness he'd used at the Hip Hop for everyone but Victoria and Jordan Baxter.

"Adam," the other man answered with a nod, not removing the matchstick he was chewing but just maneuvering it to the corner of his mouth.

"You all set to go?"

Victoria heard Adam ask that as she got out of the truck herself, realizing by then that her new husband had no intention of showing her the courtesy of opening her door.

"Yep," the other man answered, casting her a curious look as she came to stand near the right fender. "Figured I'd get you unloaded, let you know where things stand, and get outta here."

"You don't have to unload the truck. She'll do it," Adam said with a scant nod over his shoulder in Victoria's direction.

She'll do it? Victoria wondered if she'd heard correctly.

While she was still wondering, she heard Adam add, "That's why I brought her. She'll be doing all your work."

The older man raised an eyebrow but only said, "That so?"

"It is," Adam confirmed, not seeming to notice the surprise and disbelief in the other man's expression. "You can bring me up to date on what needs to be done while she hauls things in."

Victoria decided to keep as much of her dignity as she could by not showing her own shock at this dictate, raising her chin high and introducing herself. "I'm Victoria."

"I'm Sherman Broser. I usually run this here place for Adam, but he's sendin' me off to visit my daughter and grandkids. Thought it was so he could have the place to hisself for a time."

Adam didn't explain anything, even though it was clear both Victoria and his ranch foreman weren't sure what was going on. Instead he turned only slightly toward Victoria and said, "Unloading the truck is your first job as a ranch hand. Might as well get started."

And then he crossed the distance to the house, climbed the stairs and went inside.

The older man looked from Victoria to the loaded bed of the black truck to the house into which Adam had just disappeared. Victoria could tell he wasn't sure whether to follow Adam, as seemed to be indicated, or help her with the unloading.

Then, from the interior of the house, came Adam's voice. "Sherm. Let's get this done so you can be on your way."

The foreman inclined his head slightly and issued a confused-sounding chuckle before he said, "Nice meetin' ya."

"Same here," Victoria added.

And then they both went their separate ways to do Adam Benson's bidding.

"You can take the attic room. It's up those stairs there."

Victoria's suitcase had been the first thing loaded onto the truck that morning so it was the last thing she hauled into the house. By then Adam's foreman had taken his leave and Adam and Victoria were alone.

Since he'd already had her bring his bags into the bedroom to the left of the living room on the main floor, that announcement let her know she was again being dispatched to a separate bedroom.

Happy and relieved for at least that, she climbed the wooden stairs against the right wall of the living area.

The layout of the place was simple enough.

The living room and kitchen were one large room, divided only by the small rectangular table and two ladder-backed chairs that stood behind the sofa while appliances and cupboards lined the back wall.

There was a bedroom and bathroom downstairs, along with a combination mudroom-laundryroom off the kitchen with a door that opened to the backyard.

Upstairs within the steeply sloped sides of the roof was the attic bedroom Victoria had been allotted, a plain, serviceable space with a double bed, a nightstand and lamp, and a single bureau.

At least there wouldn't be much to clean, she thought as she set her suitcase on the bed, having no doubt that housekeeping would also be among the duties she'd apparently been brought to perform.

On the other hand, it wouldn't be easy to keep her distance from Adam in such close quarters, the way she was hoping to do.

Once they were both unpacked, they shared a silent meal of sandwiches and by the time that was finished the sun had set outside and Victoria was beginning to feel weighted down with Adam's studied indifference to her.

The front door was open, although it was getting too cold to be, and the night air coming through the screen and the sound of crickets seemed to beckon her outside.

It wasn't an entirely good idea, though.

Because being out in the chilly autumn air suddenly reminded her of another night. Long ago. In her father's barn. When she'd felt as if the world were her oyster, as if nothing in her life could ever go wrong, as if she could even play with fire and not get burned.

And the fire she'd decided to play with that particular night had been Adam Benson.

The son of one of her father's ranch hands. A senior in high school when she'd only been a sophomore. Tall. Dark. Heart-stoppingly handsome. But not in the same social circle as she and her friends. After all, they were Whitehorn's elite, the children of the land owners, and he was only the hired help's boy.

Victoria wasn't proud of that attitude she'd since grown out of. But that was how it was then. And in its way, it had made Adam Benson forbidden fruit.

Adam Benson, whom she'd flirted with whenever no one was looking. Whom she'd spent hours and hours secretly watching from her bedroom window as he'd worked beside his father all summer long. Adam Benson, whom she'd kept her eye on in school. Whose every move she knew, even if she didn't admit it.

Adam Benson, whom she'd found herself alone with in the barn that autumn night.

Not that he hadn't done his part.

He'd flirted right back. He'd done some showing off, the way boys do. He'd nearly singed her with deep looks that dared her to come closer.

And so, that night, when teasing and flirting and toying with each other had finally brought her to the barn to see him when she knew no one else was around, she'd let him kiss her.

Oh, had she let him kiss her...

A kiss that was not only unlike any she'd ever experienced before that—which wasn't all that much at fifteen—but a kiss that was also unlike any she'd had since.

A kiss that had ended up with them lying together in a pile of hay, clinging to each other, oblivious to anything but that kiss that had gone on and on and on…

Until her father had walked into the barn and caught them.

Never had she seen him so mad.

He'd accused Adam of all sorts of things that were much more than that simple kiss, ranting and raving and acting as if Adam were no better than a rapist, as if that's exactly what he'd have been had her father not come in when he had.

Who did Adam think he was to be pawing his daughter? her father had shouted to the rafters, enraged, appalled, red-faced with indignation and fuming more intensely than Victoria had ever seen him before.

And she hadn't had the courage to stand up to him to claim her part in that kiss.

She hadn't had the courage to stand up for Adam.

Instead she'd let her father believe the worst of him. Let her father believe she'd been the unwilling innocent young thing whom the ranch hand's son had had the audacity to maul.

It was an indefensible act of cowardice and even as it had happened, even as she'd told herself to speak up, to not let her father go on and on reaming Adam out, she'd been too afraid to do anything. Too afraid of what her father might think of her if she admitted she was every bit as responsible for the kiss as Adam had been. That Daddy's sweet little girl had courted a man—a man who was beneath her—in a barn. That she'd wanted him to kiss her. Encouraged it. Invited it. That it *had* only been a kiss.

But all the while she'd just stood there, a frozen audience to the spectacle.

And then it had gotten worse.

The whole time her father had been screaming at Adam and accusing him of all sorts of things he wasn't guilty of, she'd countered her guilt over not speaking up by telling herself that the tirade would blow over and she'd apologize to Adam later. That she'd make it up to him somehow. She hadn't even considered that her father would do anything as drastic as order Adam's entire family off the ranch.

So not only had her silence cost Adam his pride and a vicious, degrading berating he hadn't deserved, it had also cost both his parents their jobs.

And still Victoria hadn't stepped up to tell the truth.

It was a shame she'd lived with every day since, knowing she'd cost a man and woman their livelihoods to save herself.

"You're going to need to get an early start in the morning, in case you hadn't guessed."

Adam's deep voice came from behind her, from inside the house, startling her slightly from thoughts she'd been lost in.

She was hugging herself against the chilly air, staring out at the road in the distance from the front porch railing, and she didn't turn to look at him. At that moment, reliving her shame of all those years ago, she couldn't have faced him if she wanted to.

"I'll need to get an early start being the ranch hand," she said, referring to his comment to the foreman when they'd arrived.

"Ranch hand. Maid. Cook. Housecleaner. You name it, you're it."

"To put me in my place." From the lofty one she'd thought she was perched on before.

He didn't answer. He didn't need to. He'd made it clear already, with his "comeuppance" comment and his remark that morning about seeing what it was like to be from the wrong side of the tracks.

And even though it was incredibly feeble at that point, she felt the need to say, "You know, I've always regretted that night in my father's barn."

"The kiss?" Adam asked derisively.

Not the kiss. She'd never regretted the kiss.

He came to stand beside her at the porch railing, but still she didn't look at him. She kept on staring out at the countryside.

"I know—I knew even then—that I shouldn't have let my father think what he thought. That I should have told him the truth. I've always been ashamed of myself for not doing it."

"And now you think by telling me that that I'll let you off the hook? Please, spare me your apologies. Do you have any idea what you did to my family by keeping your mouth shut? It was more than getting my father fired as a ranch hand or my mother fired as your mother's maid."

"'More'?" she parroted.

"My father was a drinker. He'd dried out to get on at your place and was so happy to have a good job for a change that he was staying completely away from the booze. But after that night he went on a bender that never ended. He couldn't hold another job. Then he couldn't even get a job to lose. My mother and I had to support us. He ended up drinking himself into the grave. And all because of you. Because you thought you were too good to let your father know you were kissing me.''

"I didn't know…'' Victoria said with a catch in her voice. "I never imagined… I knew your family left Whitehorn right after that—''

"Or face your father spreading it around town that I'd attacked his daughter. He even threatened to press charges against me if we didn't. He said the only way he wouldn't ruin me for life was if we got the hell out of town.''

Every bit of Adam's fury over being misjudged rang in his voice.

No matter how lame it was, all Victoria could think to say was, "I'm so sorry.''

"You missed the best part that night,'' he went on, anyway. "After your old man sent you to the house you missed getting to see my dad grovel. Beg for another chance for us both. That wasn't pretty, let me tell you. Especially standing there knowing the whole damn time that I wasn't guilty of anything. That my family was getting raked over the coals for nothing. For something you had as much a part in as I did.''

"I know,'' she whispered miserably.

"I swore then that I'd make you pay. Someday. Somehow.''

"And now is that someday.'' She knew, in her heart, that she deserved his retribution. Deserved it even more than she'd realized before because she hadn't had any idea just how far-reaching were the consequences of that one act of cowardice on her part.

"And the somehow is that I'm going to work you like one of those lower-class people you thought you were better than. You're going to do every lousy chore I can come up with, every lousy chore you thought was beneath you—just the way you thought I was beneath you and not good enough to admit you'd been kissing willingly."

Chores. At the moment it didn't seem like much punishment for all she'd wreaked on him and his family.

"I'll do whatever work you want me to do," she told him, knowing another man might have exacted worse. Much worse than ranch- and housework. In fact, there was a part of her that welcomed whatever tasks he set so she could prove to him that she really did have more character than she'd exhibited so many years ago. So she could make amends. So she could show him—and maybe herself, too—that she was made of stronger stuff.

"I know you won't believe this, but I'm not the same person I was twenty years ago," she said then, quietly. "I hated myself for being too weak to stand up to my father."

"Sure you did," Adam said facetiously.

Victoria finally got up the nerve to look at him, directly at eyes that were shadowed and yet still seemed able to bore right through her.

"I really am sorry. Truly, truly sorry."

They stood there, staring at each other in the autumn moonlight, and Victoria could see a muscle in Adam's jaw clenching and unclenching in long-held anger.

But even so, somewhere along the line, the air around them seemed to change. Seemed to charge with the same kind of electrical energy that had been between them so many years ago. On a night like this one. When he'd kissed her.

And Victoria suddenly remembered that kiss much, much too vividly.

She remembered big, strong arms coming around her. Powerful hands gently pressing against her back to bring her nearer. That handsome face slowly easing downward. Warm lips meeting hers in a split second that ended almost before she knew it had begun. Testing the waters to see if he was welcome.

And he had been welcome. So welcome she'd raised her chin to let him know it, allowing easier access to a mouth that was eager for the real thing. For a real kiss. From him.

And then he'd given her that real kiss. Softly, tenderly, at first. Teaching a little because she was pretty inexperienced. But savoring, too. Making her feel so wonderful she wanted to go on kissing him the rest of her life.

Was she mistaken or was his face a little closer now, too?

She wasn't mistaken.

With his eyes still holding hers, he'd actually leaned in slightly, just the way he had that other night....

Was he going to kiss her?

Victoria couldn't believe it. Not after the way he'd acted since yesterday. Not after all he'd said just now.

But there he was, closer still. So close she could see him more clearly even in the darkness. So close she could smell the scent of his after-shave again. So close she could feel the warmth of his breath.

And she was raising her chin, too. Allowing him access even as a voice in the back of her mind demanded to know what on earth she was doing.

Then he straightened. As if he hadn't done anything at all.

And he sneered at her.

"Not much fun to be teased, is it?" he said, just before turning on his heels and going back inside, leaving her hanging. And feeling like a fool.

So the payback wasn't only going to be in working her like a ranch hand, she thought. It was going to be in humiliating her, too.

And she did feel humiliated because the full impact of that almost-kiss still lingered inside her along with the embarrassment of knowing she'd have met it, returned it, maybe even liked it.

But humiliation was payback she also had coming, she reminded herself.

And again she thought that it could have been worse.

Although at that moment, with lips dry from unquenched thirst, standing there awash in old shame and regret, and in her newest humiliation, the fact that her comeuppance could have been more harsh wasn't much comfort.

Three

"I'm going to have to talk to you later about all this," Adam said snappishly into the telephone late the next morning.

It wasn't that his assistant on the other end of the call had done anything wrong. Adam was angry and disgusted with himself. With his own inability to keep his mind on track when he was trying to do business. Or any other time in the past two days for that matter.

He'd set Victoria to the task of cleaning the cabin from top to bottom while he appropriated the desk in the corner of the living room for his office. That was where the phone was, so he'd opted for putting his laptop computer, printer and fax machine there, too.

But the simple wire connections had taken him more than an hour and there wasn't a single one he'd hooked up right on the first try.

Thanks to Victoria.

Secondhand clothes did not detract anything from her appeal. The plain, loose-fitting jeans and over-size, faded red sweatshirt she had on certainly should have made her less of a distraction. At least he thought they should.

But had they?

No, they hadn't.

In fact the big sweatshirt only made him strain all the more for a glimpse of her breasts hiding beneath it. And every time she bent over, those damn jeans just enticed him to look at her perfect little rump.

Suddenly mergers and acquisitions and bottom lines and anything going bust developed completely new meanings for him, creating uninvited images in his mind that had nothing whatsoever to do with business.

So, after his second stammer over ass…ets, he'd had to end the call that was supposed to have accomplished much more than it had.

Now here he was, sitting with the chair at a sideways angle to the desk, papers in hand, still staring surreptitiously at that derriere of hers as she crawled on her hands and knees to scoop ashes from the fireplace. And although this whole deal had been intended as payback for her, it seemed to be turning into punishment for him.

Punishment today. Punishment last night.

Last night.

Just the thought made him want to kick himself. It had made him want to kick himself every time— about a dozen of them—that it popped back into his mind to taunt him.

He should never have gone out onto that porch with her. He should have stayed right where he was—inside. Even if he hadn't been able to keep himself from watching her through the screen. At least then he'd had a physical distance from her even if he hadn't had much of a distance from her mentally.

But had he stayed inside? Had he been *able* to stay inside and resist the allure of her?

No.

He'd been drawn outside in spite of telling himself not to go. In spite of knowing he shouldn't go. In spite of every ounce of wisdom he possessed screaming for him not to go.

And what had happened as a result?

He'd damn near kissed her, that's what.

Kissed her.

As if he didn't already know what kind of fresh hell *that* could stir up.

Sure, he'd managed to stop himself before it was too late and he'd actually made any kind of contact. And, yes, he'd covered his tracks, pretending that it had been something he'd planned to do to taunt her. But that had only been an act. The truth was, something had come over him that he'd been almost powerless to control.

Seeing her out in the moonlight like that. Talking about that night in her father's barn so long ago. Remembering what it had been like to finally have her in his arms after daydreaming about it, fantasizing about it, wanting it for what had seemed like an eternity to a seventeen-year-old kid.

But he couldn't lose sight of how that kiss had ended, he reminded himself all over again. He couldn't lose sight of what she'd done, or hadn't done. Of the damage her silence had caused to his whole family.

He owed it to his father, to his mother, to himself, to make her pay for that silence, that damage. For the bitter taste that kiss had left him with.

But he was beginning to think that resisting her in the process might be one of the hardest things he'd ever have to do. After all, he hadn't been able to stop himself from going outside to be with her the night before. And he was having one hell of a time keeping his eyes off her now, off her hair all tied up into a knot of curls at the top of her head. Off her cheeks flush with work. Off that rear end his hands were itching to reach out for.

But resist her he would, he swore as he realized his thoughts and eyes were taking yet another stroll in her direction.

Because no apologies—no matter how heartfelt she made them sound—no beautiful face or enchanting eyes or great body, were enough to make up for what she'd done.

He was going to make sure she paid for it.

And if, in the meantime, he had to toss and turn in his bed at night, remembering that brief moment twenty years ago when he'd held her, kissed her, lost himself in the sweet velvet of her mouth, if in the meantime he had to wage war with his own wandering thoughts and unwelcome desires, then that's what he'd do.

He'd toss and turn and wage that war.

But he'd have his due.

It just wouldn't be easy denying the part of him that seemed to be wanting more than that.

* * *

Victoria didn't mind doing the housework Adam assigned her as much as she minded doing it with him watching her. What did he think she was going to do if he turned his back? Sit down and eat bonbons?

It was just so annoying. And unnerving.

She tried to ignore it. To ignore him. To seem as if she wasn't even aware of it.

But, boy, was she aware of it!

Aware of him.

It didn't help that he was dressed the way he had been most of the time when he'd worked beside his father. Not only did seeing him like that stir up old memories, old appreciations, but now he filled out his blue jeans a whole lot better than he had then. Not to mention that the tan Western-style shirt he wore with the sleeves rolled up to expose those ultra-sexy forearms and wrists also stretched across his broad shoulders, chest and back like a loving caress and barely contained the bulge of his biceps.

And if that wasn't enough, there was even something arousing about the masculine sight of his big feet in snakeskin cowboy boots instead of the Italian dress shoes he'd worn the day of their wedding.

Arousing? Had she thought he was arousing?

She hadn't meant that.

How could someone so contrary be arousing? Regardless of what he had on or how he looked?

So what if his black hair was still as perfect as if an expensive stylist had cut it that very morning?

Perfection only made him seem all the more unapproachable.

So what if she noticed all over again each time she looked at him how incredibly handsome were his strong, chiseled features?

He still couldn't look at her without frowning so darkly his face turned into an ominous storm cloud.

So what if she'd lain awake in bed most of the night before wondering what things might be like between them if the fiasco in her father's barn had never happened? If Adam's family had just moved away on their own and now she and Adam had both returned to Whitehorn coincidentally at the same time?

That wasn't the reality of things.

So what if she'd spent until the wee hours of this morning imagining them encountering each other at the Hip Hop Café? Their glances meeting, a split second of perplexity mingled with interest in those pewter-gray eyes of his before it dawned on him who she was and his supple mouth stretched into a grin that let her know how glad he was to see her?

That wasn't what had happened. He knew exactly who she was, didn't like her, and was more likely to snarl at her than smile.

So what if she'd imagined him casting her one of those I-dare-you-to-come-closer looks that had been so intriguing when they were adolescents, a look she couldn't resist, a look she wouldn't have had to resist now? A look that might have brought them together and been only the beginning of them talking the whole night through, catching up, finding that all those same sparks from years ago could be reignited?

Now the only challenge in his expression dared her to defy his orders, decrees and demands.

So what if she'd pictured them coming to this cozy little cabin under other circumstances—to spend some time alone, getting to know each other in a way they never had before? Discovering that that childish attraction could blossom into something much more? Something that was meant to be, that had always been meant to be?

No matter what she pictured in her mind, the only reason they were at the cabin was so that he could work her like a dog.

So what if she'd recalled those few moments on the porch the night before but put a different spin on them, imagining Adam following her outside, coming up from behind her to wrap his arms around her so he could chase away the chill, propping his chin atop her head, teasing her kindly, devilishly?

The truth was that he'd come out onto the porch only to be nasty to her, to throw her apology back in her face, to let her know just what a horrible thing she'd done in allowing her father to believe the worst of him.

So what if her fantasy had been so vivid she could feel herself leaning back against his muscular body, trusting him, enjoying the feel of safety and security and sensuality all rolled up in strong arms and powerful hands that only touched her with the utmost tenderness?

The truth was that he hadn't touched her at all, let alone with tenderness. And as for feeling safe or secure when she was anywhere around him? Fat chance of that!

So what if she'd seen herself turning in those arms to look up into his moon-gilded features, tilting her chin just as he dipped his downward to press his lips against hers exactly the way she remembered from her father's barn?

This time he'd only made it seem as if he might be about to kiss her so that he could pull back and make her feel like an idiot for anticipating it, for not rejecting him first and making it clear she had no intention of letting him kiss her now or ever, whether they were married or not.

So what if, in her mind, he'd carried her back inside the cabin, to his room, to his bed—

Victoria shook her head, trying to rid herself of this back-and-forth reverie and the path it was taking before it went all the way to where it had gone in the early hours of the morning.

So what, so what, so what…?

So what good did it do her to even think about things being different than they were?

No good at all.

In fact just imagining it had made her heart pound, last night and again now, and there wasn't anything good about that.

It was even worse than having to work under Adam's scrutiny.

Besides, it wasn't as if she wanted any of those so-whats to be true. She could have lived her whole life perfectly happy with never having laid eyes on him again.

It was just that since she had laid eyes on him again it could have been so much nicer if things were different.

She cast Adam a quick glance, hoping he might have finally stopped staring at her.

He hadn't.

And he was scowling again. As if she'd done something wrong.

Or maybe he could somehow tell what she'd been thinking just by looking at her.

Victoria could feel her face heat even at the impossible prospect of that.

Wouldn't he just love to know what had been going through her mind! Wouldn't it boost his ego and his enjoyment at her expense a hundredfold?

But of course he couldn't read her thoughts, she assured herself. He had no way of knowing what had just been on her mind.

She was grateful for that.

Because she'd never give him the satisfaction of knowing she would even entertain a notion of him as anything but the bane of her current existence. She certainly wouldn't allow him again what she'd allowed him on the porch the evening before when she'd made it seem as if she might have let him kiss her.

Maybe she'd had to marry him. Maybe she had to do his bidding. But she didn't have to let him know he could stir up anything in her except maybe contempt. He certainly didn't have to know she ever had any thoughts of him as an attractive, sexy, arousing—

There was that arousing business again.

Once more it set off an alarm inside her that made her shy away from the very idea.

She might have to play this game of his but she didn't have to let the man himself get to her, she told herself sternly.

Every time anything remotely positive or alluring or enticing or engaging went through her head she vowed that she'd remind herself that he was a man who had forced her to marry him. He was a man who had threatened her family's well-being. He was a man who was delighting in working her unmercifully.

He was a man who hated her. Who had seen the worst of her, wouldn't forget it, wanted to rub her nose in it, and certainly wouldn't forgive it.

Okay, so that part chafed and haunted her when she would much rather her cowardice of so long ago be forgiven and left in the past.

But he was going to make sure that didn't happen and she had to accept it as the consequence of her actions.

As a consequence of his actions, she wasn't going to let herself be attracted to the man who wouldn't forget or forgive. Let alone allow anything akin to arousal.

As far as she was concerned, he was the ogre refusing her passage across the bridge that would put her greatest shame behind her.

And that was just how she was going to think of him.

Except that as she finished cleaning out the firebox

and stood with the bucket of ashes, she caught sight of him again. In all his masculine glory.

Adam Benson was no ogre. He was drop-dead gorgeous and could make her blood race through her veins as easily now as he could when she was fifteen.

Then he barked, "When you're finished in here you can take the ladder out of the barn and pick the last of the apples off that tree out back. I'll have apple pie for dessert tonight. You do know how to make an apple pie, don't you? Or didn't the prima donna ever learn to cook?"

"I can make an apple pie," she answered flatly, feeling her blood slow its pace.

"Good. Then do it."

Victoria didn't answer that. She merely went to dump the ashes in the trash, thinking that maybe she didn't have to try so hard to fight images of him as an appealing man.

Maybe she just had to open her eyes.

Dinner that evening was meat loaf, potatoes, rolls and salad, with the freshly baked apple pie waiting on the counter and the cabin bathed in silence.

Unfortunately that silence left Victoria thinking too much about her own misery and what had caused it.

High up in the apple tree she'd accidentally encountered a beehive. Even a fast retreat down the ladder hadn't kept her from being stung several time on the face, ears, neck, arms and hands. As she sat through the evening meal she was all too aware of the itching, burning agony of the welts that had grown to full cherry size and were almost as red.

She'd hoped her late-day shower and shampoo would help, but instead the welts just seemed to be worse and she could hardly keep from fidgeting as she sat across the small dinner table from Adam, trying to scratch without causing herself even more pain.

For his part, Adam had gone from staring at her while she cleaned the cabin to acting as if she were invisible since her return from apple picking. So he didn't notice either the red marks or her attempts to alleviate her own discomfort. Instead he had his nose buried in a computer printout as he ate.

Only when she set a slice of the pie in front of him did he put aside his paperwork and look up at her.

Well, not all the way up immediately.

First his gaze hit her at waist level where she had the purple shirt she'd brought with her from home tucked into a fresh pair of her new hand-me-down jeans. Then his gray eyes slowly raised, stalling over her breasts for a split second, before going all the way to her face.

That put the scowl back in his expression.

"Have you broken out in spots?" he asked, taking a closer look, as if he couldn't quite believe what he was seeing.

"Bee stings. There's a hive in the apple tree."

Victoria had her hair pulled loosely at the base of her neck and tied with a scarf to keep it behind her ears so it didn't irritate the bites. She reached gingerly to rub the welt on her left lobe that almost gave the appearance of an earring.

But if there was a positive side to this it was that the revelation of her beehive encounter to Adam seemed to have knocked him slightly for a loop. Because unless she was misreading the change in his expression, he hadn't purposely sent her to be stung and, in fact, was as surprised as she'd been that the hive was out there. She thought she might even be looking at the evidence of some feelings of guilt for having sent her anywhere near it.

"What did you do?" he asked in the first civil tone of voice he'd used.

"I got down as fast as I could and ran."

He actually cracked a small smile, apparently at the thought of her retreat. Which, now that she thought about it, had had some comical elements to it.

"Looks like you didn't run fast enough."

"I don't know. I ran pretty fast. Most of them got me before I actually realized what was happening."

"You look awful."

"Gee, thanks. Just the look I was going for."

"I meant that you look like it *feels* awful," he amended as she carefully scratched a sting on her jaw. "Did you get all the stingers out?"

"Was I supposed to? I've never been stung before."

He rolled his eyes. "That figures. I forgot you were a hothouse flower."

Victoria did not welcome the return of his facetiousness so she didn't respond to it.

Adam sighed then, as if giving in to something. ''You'd better let me take a look at them and see if there are stingers to get rid of. If you leave them in they're apt to get infected. Besides, if you get the stingers out, those bumps will be gone by tomorrow.''

''I'd appreciate it, then,'' she said formally. Not because she was putting on airs but because the thought of him close to her, touching her made her stomach suddenly jittery.

''Why don't you eat your pie and I'll get the supper mess cleared. Then we can do it.''

That last part had sounded more suggestive than she'd intended. She could feel herself blushing.

''What I mean is—''

He stopped her mid-explanation. ''I know what you mean.''

While he took the initial forkful of his pie she used the opportunity to clear the table. Truth was she wanted some distance from him and her own embarrassment.

''Pretty good pie,'' he commented from behind her about the time she reached the sink.

First a smile and a nicer tone, and now a compliment? She'd never known her meat loaf to be the cure-all for contrariness but maybe she should reassess it, she thought.

''Don't sound so amazed,'' she countered a bit more flirtatiously than she'd meant to.

''That Victoria Rutherford can bake? I *am* amazed.''

He said her name as if even that was a burr under

his saddle, and she hated the sound of it. "These days some people call me Tori."

But his only answer was a flat, "Do they." And she could tell he had no intention of using the shorter, warmer version of her name.

So much for that, she thought, slightly embarrassed once again at having her overture rejected.

As she rinsed the dishes and put them in the dishwasher that came with the small but fully equipped kitchen, Adam brought his pie with him to eat standing beside her.

He leaned his jeans-clad rear against the counter, his long legs stretched out and crossed nonchalantly at the ankles, and Victoria wished she wasn't so aware of the pure potency of his masculinity.

But no amount of trying to ignore it made her any less aware. Or any less affected by it. Every sense seemed to stand up and take notice of him.

He finished his pie and put his plate in the dishwasher. "I'll see if I can round up what I need and we'll get started," he said, pushing off the counter and leaving on long strides that made his heels click against the wooden floor until he reached the rug that covered it in the living room section of the space. Then the clicks resumed as he went into the hall that led to the bathroom.

Victoria couldn't have been more attuned to those steps if she'd been watching him take them. So much so that she felt something inside her grow with each one.

Anticipation? she wondered.

Possibly.

Anticipation and something else.

Eagerness? Maybe even some light shade of excitement?

But that was crazy.

Poking around with a needle and tweezers in welts that were already sore was hardly something to be excited about.

It was the thought of Adam getting close to her. Touching her.

Stop it! she ordered herself. He's an ogre. An ogre. An ogre.

Except that he didn't look like an ogre when she turned to find him standing there, supplies in hand.

There was nothing ogreish about his heart-stoppingly handsome face or his big man's body or the impact it all had on her.

"Why don't you lie down on the couch?" he suggested. "That way I can have the lamplight shining right on you and you'll be less likely to make any sudden movements."

Victoria's mouth went dry at the idea of lying on the sofa with him above her. *Close* above her…

No matter how reasonable his directions were, it didn't help the thrumming of her pulse.

"Do you want me to do this or not?" Adam asked at her hesitation.

Maybe it was better to suffer and risk infection, Victoria thought.

But she knew that wasn't true.

"I suppose it needs to be done," she answered, hoping it sounded as if she was leery of the pain and not of being near him.

"Get some ice. I won't hurt you any more than I have to," he said reassuringly.

But at that moment, under those circumstances, she almost wished for his sarcasm and hostility instead. At least when he was off-putting it was easier to resist the other things going on inside her.

Now, being nice, his appeal was lethal.

"Just let me get a drink of water," she said, buying herself time and hoping it would stave off the dryness in her mouth and somehow help her regain her equilibrium.

But filling a glass with tap water and drinking it took only a few seconds. And the water didn't help. Her mouth still felt like the Sahara desert and as for regaining her equilibrium, water just wasn't strong enough to accomplish that.

She had no choice then but to make an ice pack and return to where Adam sat on the coffee table, waiting for her.

"I burned the needle with a match and then cleaned it with some alcohol," he told her.

For a moment she stood in front of the couch, looking at it, at Adam sitting right there, barely a foot away from where he expected her to lie down.

But she didn't want to make him mad so she tried to ignore the jitters in her stomach and the race of her pulse, and forced herself to sit first and then slowly stretch out on the cushions in front of him.

"Should we start at the top and work down?" he asked.

Visions of things that were a whole lot more sensual than taking stingers out of bee bites flashed through Victoria's mind.

But all she said was, "Sure. Whatever you want. I mean, think. Whatever you think."

He took the makeshift ice pack from her and placed it on the welt at her right temple, leaning to study more closely what he'd be tending.

"You know, I wouldn't have sent you out there to pick those apples if I'd have known about the hive. I didn't mean for you to get stung."

Was that an apology? From Adam Benson?

Victoria could hardly believe what she was hearing.

"It's okay," she said, keeping to her decision to not try engaging him in too much conversation and leaving the talking to him.

"It's a good thing you weren't allergic like one of my half brothers," he continued. "He ended up in the hospital."

So he was suffering some guilt. Good. She was glad to know he had at least that much of a conscience.

"I'm lucky," she agreed. Although at that moment lucky was not how she felt.

Hot was more like it.

Not that the room was excessively warm. In fact, the front door was ajar the way it had been the previous night and the evening air was very cool. But Adam seemed to give off heat on his own.

Or maybe it was just her own body's reaction to him.

But either way, even the ice pack on her head wasn't cooling her off.

"Why don't you hold that on your ear next, and I'll get going here," he suggested, bending so far over her his nose couldn't have been more than two inches from her face.

She could smell the clean, citrusy scent of his after-shave and it suddenly made her head go so light she felt dizzy.

How was she going to lie there perfectly still and pretend he didn't have a physical effect on her when she was reeling with physical effects?

"So what kind of life did I steal you away from?" he asked then, interrupting her thoughts just as he wielded the tweezers.

She wondered if he was only trying to distract her, or if he gave a tinker's damn what kind of life he'd taken her from.

"I went to Boston University after graduating high school, got my bachelor's degree and then my master's there."

"And stuck around to work there, too?"

"That's about the size of it."

"As a professor?"

"I'm not a full professor yet. But I teach philosophy, yes."

"Philosophy?"

"Mainly women's studies."

"You're a feminist," he said as if it amused him.

"I believe in equal rights and privileges for everyone, if that's what you mean."

"Really?" he said facetiously again, and she knew she'd touched a nerve once more.

"All right, look, I admit that I was a snob as a kid. Does that make you happy?"

"But now you aren't, is that what you expect me to believe?"

"I'm definitely not a snob now, but you can believe it or not, I don't care."

That was a lie. She did care. Once she'd gotten out into the world she'd realized just how elitist she'd been. And it wasn't something she was proud of. She'd worked hard to shed that old sense of superiority and opened her eyes to the way things should be between people.

She wished Adam could see that. Could see that she was different than that obnoxious young girl who had turned her nose up at the ranch hand's son in public all the while she'd been secretly lusting after him in private.

She hazarded a glance up at Adam and discovered him smiling slightly again, as if he was enjoying taunting her and her reaction to it.

"Got it!" he said then, pulling out something with the tweezers that was too small for her to see.

He wiped them on a tissue and then took her hand and the ice pack with it away from her ear to focus on the sting on her cheekbone.

Victoria wished he hadn't done that.

The touch of his hand on hers sent wild things bolting up her whole arm and all through her like an electrical shock. And worse than that, she felt her nipples harden in response—something that she knew was all too visible in the shirt pulled tight across her breasts.

She prayed Adam wouldn't look down and notice.

But her prayers weren't answered.

As he reached for the needle again she saw him catch sight of her chest and she wanted to crawl in a hole.

Instead she pretended her arm was tired and switched hands to hold the ice pack with her right hand so she could cross her arm over her breasts.

It was hardly a subtle move and it brought a soft chuckle from Adam, as if he saw right through it.

''Maybe we should shut the door. It's getting a little chilly in here,'' she said, again lying, but hoping to fool him.

He got up without commenting and closed the door.

And Victoria did the dumbest thing: she watched him do it.

Her gaze rode along on the back pockets of his jeans and the sight of that to-die-for derriere didn't help matters. Not at all. In fact, it made them worse still as her nipples seemed to tighten up even more.

And once again her mouth went dry and her brain tormented her with images of his hands on her breasts as hers reached around him and learned if his rear end felt as good as it looked.

She closed her eyes and willed her body and mind to behave. But it was a struggle and when she opened her eyes again Adam was back, sitting on the coffee table, looking so incredibly handsome that her heart skipped a beat and she completely lost the battle.

"Are you ready?" he asked.

Ready for what—that was more the question.

But Victoria said a feeble, "Sure," hating that it came out on a squeak of a voice.

He bent to his task and said, "A teacher's salary can't keep you living in the style you were accustomed to. Was Daddy supplementing your income before things tightened up for him?"

That helped, because Victoria took offense. As it almost seemed she was meant to.

"I've supported myself since graduating from college," she announced tersely, feeling the pure sensuality he'd roused in her abate somewhat.

"Not living on Beacon Hill, then, are you?"

"I have a perfectly nice apartment near the school."

"Alone?"

He seemed to be fishing with that question and if he was asking if she was involved with anyone she wasn't going to give him the satisfaction he was looking for. Instead she gave only a simple, "Yes, alone."

He extracted another stinger and reached for her hand to move the ice pack again.

But this time Victoria pulled her hand away before he could touch her and said curtly, "Where do you want this?"

Adam smiled, a full-out grin this time. "That sounded like a threat."

"I just meant—"

"I know what you meant," he repeated, making

an elaborate point of aiming just one extended index finger at the spot where she should hold the ice.

Victoria found it without more assistance from him, stared up at the ceiling as if nothing at all was going on with her, and hazarded a question of her own. "Where do you live?"

He went back to work before he said, "I have a place in Manhattan and another one in Chicago and Denver and L.A. A condo in Aspen. A flat in London. This ranch. And now yours, too. At one time or another I live in all of them."

"And a share in the Kincaid spread if that goes through," she reminded him, rather than taking the bait that seemed to have been in his tone when he'd included her family's ranch in his list of holdings. "You get around," she added then.

"Out of necessity."

He moved on to another sting, again merely pointing to where she should hold the ice pack next.

"And your mother?" she asked, referring to his aunt Gertrude who had raised him. "Where is she now?"

"She passed away last year. Heart attack. She went quick."

"I'm sorry."

"So am I."

Again he finished with one of the bites, let her know where to move the ice, and studied the one she'd just numbed.

"What about your work now?" he asked, changing the heavier tone they'd drifted into. "Did they expect you back today?"

"I took the semester off to deal with selling the ranch and moving everything out so my mother wouldn't have to leave Dad to do it."

"So you won't be missed."

"What about you? Will you be missed at work?"

She was fishing because she didn't know exactly what he did for a living. She assumed it was business of some sort, a business that obviously paid well and for which he traveled a great deal. But since he acted as if it was a given that she knew what his occupation was, she was afraid he would treat her like a dimwit if she asked outright.

But the fishing didn't help because all he said in answer to her question was, "I *am* work."

"Does that mean everything stops while you're away?" She tried again.

"It means that where I am is where the work is."

And that seemed to be that because when he'd finished with the welt on her jaw and moved on to the one on her neck he said, "I think this is the last," as if the previous subject was played out. "And the worst."

"I know."

"It almost looks like there's two stingers in it."

"A mutant bee?"

He laughed. "Maybe. Turn your head a little, will you? The shadow of your jaw makes it hard to see."

She did as she was told, trying not to be as thrilled as she was by just the simple fact that he was being nice.

"So what's on my agenda for tomorrow?" she asked as she stared at the cushions of the sofa back, wanting to remind herself that he really was the tyrant in this piece.

"One side of the barn is showing more weather damage than the rest. You get to scrape it and paint it," he answered as if he was granting a favor.

"Oh, good," she said with a fair amount of facetiousness of her own.

"Better check around for hornet or wasp nests in the eaves before you get started. I don't want a repeat of this."

"Don't worry."

Neither of them said anything else for a while. Victoria just stayed staring at the plaid pattern of the couch while Adam worked on her.

It was a relief to know this whole thing was nearly over with, and yet there was a part of her that was almost sorry.

Certainly it hadn't been pleasant but she and Adam had actually had a normal conversation and that had been nice. Nicer than any of the rest of the time they'd spent together since they'd met up again.

Maybe it was her long day's work catching up with her and the fatigue it brought with it, but she suddenly found herself relaxing.

She felt him pull out the stingers and expected him to pronounce her finished, to get up and away from her as soon as he could. But he was still sitting there, leaning over her.

"Are you done?" she asked, still facing the sofa back.

But his only answer was a husky, "Mmm."

She took that for a yes and turned her head.

But Adam still didn't sit back. He went on leaning forward, his legs spread apart, his elbows on his knees, looking at her from beneath a frown that was somehow different from his usual scowl.

She thought he was still studying the sting on the side of her neck. But then she realized his gaze wasn't quite that high.

Instead it was on her breasts.

He raised it then, though not in any hurry. To the hollow of her throat. To her chin.

To her lips.

But there were no stings anywhere near her lips. So what was he looking at?

But she knew.

It was in the air around them just the way it had been the night before, out on the porch.

He was making it seem as if he might kiss her.

But this time Victoria swore she wouldn't be duped. She was wise to his game. He'd wait for her to respond, to invite the kiss, and then he'd pull back.

So she should pull back first, she told herself. She shouldn't do anything to invite or even welcome him. She should sneer. Turn her head away. Sit up and get off that couch to make it clear kissing him was not part of the deal.

But did she do that? Any of it?

No, she didn't.

She just couldn't.

She didn't tilt her chin the way she had for him the previous night. But she didn't avert her face, either. She didn't even sit up the way she knew she should to get out of harm's way.

She didn't do anything at all.

He did, though.

This time he actually did kiss her.

It took her completely by surprise. In fact, it shocked her so much she almost didn't kiss him back.

Almost.

But then there she was, returning the kiss, enjoying it, savoring it.

Even as a part of her knew she should push him away, there was still a little voice from deep in the back of her head that rejoiced, *I'm kissing Adam Benson!*

But then it was over almost before it had begun.

He reared back as if he'd surprised himself as much as her. As if he was just as shocked.

He stood abruptly. Almost angrily.

But when he spoke—despite the fact that his voice was deep and raspy—his anger didn't seem aimed at her.

"Make a paste of baking soda and water and dot it on the stings," he instructed.

"Okay," she said, somewhat stunned.

Then he left her sitting there.

He went straight to his room and closed the door.

And tonight Victoria had the sense that even though he'd left her feeling all wound up and confused and vaguely disappointed, the torment of that kiss had all been his.

Four

Adam was up at sunrise the next morning after another restless night. But he didn't wake Victoria. He wanted some time to himself first. To get his bearings.

Not that it would last, he knew. Because the minute she was awake and anywhere around, he'd be thrown off course just the way he had been since laying eyes on her on Saturday. But he needed to at least feel as if he had some control.

For even just a half hour or so, anyway.

Until she came down those stairs from the attic and everything got all jumbled again.

It was as if she could cast some kind of spell over him. Without even trying, he thought as he plugged in the coffeepot.

Of course it didn't help that he'd felt guilty as hell the evening before when he'd realized that she'd been so badly stung.

She'd looked miserable with those bee stings like polka dots marring her ordinarily flawless skin. And to have someone poking around in them with a needle? He wasn't a big fan of needles, so he'd sympathized.

None of it had been in his plan, that was for sure.

He hadn't meant to cause her any kind of physical pain when he'd opted for this course of action. His idea of comeuppance didn't involve any more than maybe the sore muscles that came from hard work. He never would have sent her out to pick those apples if he'd known about the hive.

So guilt and sympathy, added to her usual effect on him, had really thrown him off, he reasoned to explain his friendlier attitude toward her.

Or so he wanted to believe.

He poured himself a cup of the coffee he'd just made and took it with him to the big picture window that looked out onto the front porch and gave him a view of the dawn's splendor of yellow and pink cotton-candy haze.

But if he were honest with himself he had to admit that his friendlier attitude hadn't only come out of guilt and sympathy and her usual effect on him.

There was also a part of him—a part he wished he could get rid of—that didn't like the way she acted around him.

Skittish. Nervous. Uncomfortable.

That was the Victoria Rutherford he was faced with now. And it should have fit right into his plans because years ago, when she'd held all the cards, that was how he'd felt.

But now that the shoe was on the other foot, he didn't like it. He didn't like that she kept a cautious eye on him, as if she were watching a stormy summer sky. He didn't like that she seemed leery of opening her mouth to speak. He didn't even like that she gave him such a wide berth—although that was something that was likely for the best.

But the part of him that didn't like the way she acted around him was probably just ego, he told himself.

After all, there was no doubt that the Victoria Rutherford of years ago had been more of a boost to his self-esteem. Back then she'd cast him secret glances. She'd granted him coy smiles behind everyone else's backs. She'd watched with eyes that sparkled with enticement. She'd flirted with him outrageously when no one was looking. And she'd purposely put herself in positions where they might run into each other.

That had definitely been more flattering than having her watching him now as if she were afraid of him.

He was beginning to feel like the Beast to her Beauty.

Of course that was what he'd set himself up for. That was basically what he'd thought he wanted.

But somehow it still ate at him.

Maybe because it didn't take away what made this whole situation the most difficult. It didn't take away the attraction that one glance at her, or even just knowing she was in close proximity, brought to life in him.

She was just too damn tempting.

It put him on a seesaw—one minute hating her for what she'd done when they were teenagers, the next not hating her. Worse than that, not wanting her to hate him. And worse still, noticing how sweet her hair smelled or how tendrils of it curled around the base of her neck when she tied it up on top of her head. Noticing how much softer her features were when he wasn't such a bear and she relaxed a little. Noticing how those big blue eyes of hers sparkled when she wasn't wary of him. How satiny her skin was and the way her throat dipped gracefully into the hollow. And then there were her lips....

They'd been his downfall the night before.

It had been tough enough being as close to her as he'd been when he'd pulled the stingers out, but getting to that last one and having her turn her head had put just the right curve to her neck. A curve that had stirred him up inside and left him wanting to kiss it so much it had almost driven him crazy.

And then when she'd swiveled her head back again and his gaze had settled on those lush lips of hers?

He'd been a goner.

But kissing her?

What the hell had he been thinking?

He hadn't been thinking, that was the problem.

In fact, it almost seemed as if he'd blacked out for a split second and come to to find his mouth pressed to hers.

Even as he was in the middle of kissing her, he hadn't been able to believe he'd given in to the very thing that had gotten him into trouble before.

But damn if he hadn't.

And for the same reason he had years ago. He just couldn't *not* kiss her.

It hadn't been any different in her father's barn

that night. He'd known she was off-limits. Out of his league. She was the boss's daughter.

But he hadn't been able to keep any of that in mind when she'd come closer and closer. When she'd smiled at him. Flirted with him. Let him know she was as interested in him as he was in her.

But she hadn't smiled at him last night. She hadn't flirted. She hadn't shown any interest at all. Yet he'd still kissed her.

That made this time worse than the last.

Although she did *kiss you back,* a little voice in his head reminded him.

For only a brief moment. But she'd damn well kissed him.

He'd been the one to end it—that should count for something, shouldn't it?

But it didn't.

How could it when the fact of the matter was he'd started it?

And he'd liked it.

He'd liked it so much that temptation had sky-rocketed and he could have gone on kissing her and touching her and—

Adam closed his eyes and willed his body to stop the reaction it was having to just the thoughts running through his head.

The memories.

The yearning for more than memories....

He opened his eyes in a hurry before the images that were popping into his mind got too much of a stronghold and only made things worse.

What kind of payback was it if he fell for her? he

asked himself as sternly as he would a willfully lazy employee.

None at all, was the answer.

But the trouble was that over the years he'd forgotten how appealing Victoria could be. He'd concentrated on that one act she'd perpetrated. He'd focused on that and, lo and behold, she'd become the evil witch he'd thought her for so long. An evil witch he wouldn't have any trouble getting back at when the opportunity arose.

But now here she was in living color and that harsh light had somehow softened. And he was having one hell of a time trying to not enjoy her. Trying to fight what seemed to come naturally such as talking to her, getting to know her again, kissing her....

Having her kiss him back....

The pleasure he took in this was supposed to be in the comeuppance. In seeing her work like a ranch hand or a maid. In watching her bristle at having to dirty her hands.

The pleasure was not supposed to be in other things, other moments, like last night. The pleasure was not supposed to be in her.

But he didn't know how to stop it. He'd tried to keep in mind what she'd done. He'd tried to remember all the reasons he'd come to hate her.

They just didn't make any difference. They didn't stop him from lighting up inside at the sight of her. From craving the sound of her voice. From itching to be with her every minute he wasn't.

So he'd have to deal with it, he decided. What else could he do? He'd already started this and he had to see it through to the end. He'd just have to fight what she brought to life in him in the meantime.

And if he enjoyed his time with her a little? If he enjoyed *her* a little?

He sure as hell wasn't going to let her know it.

And he sure as hell wasn't going to kiss her again.

He closed his eyes once more, this time shaking his head, too. At himself. At the desire he had even at that moment to climb the steps to the attic room and wake her with a better kiss than they'd shared on the couch.

Everything he'd just hashed through, everything he'd just told himself, didn't have much impact on that desire.

Willpower, he thought, I have to have willpower.

He just didn't know if there was enough willpower in the world to get him through this without giving in to Victoria Rutherford's pull on him.

Victoria wasn't too sure what she was going to find when she went downstairs that morning. Since she'd awakened on her own at the crack of dawn rather than having Adam as her gruff alarm, she had nothing with which to gauge his mood as she got dressed. And after that kiss the night before and his abrupt disappearance into his bedroom, she couldn't even begin to guess what she might be confronted with today.

Since she'd had his advance warning that she was to paint the barn, she put on the most worn of her used clothes—a plain, faded sweatshirt and a pair of stained jeans.

She caught her hair into a ponytail, did a quick makeup job that only involved blush and a little mascara, and then she ventured toward the stairs, half thinking that Adam might not yet be up since she hadn't heard any sounds downstairs.

He was up, though.

She spotted him as she hit the third step. He was standing at the picture window with a cup of coffee in one hand, staring outside.

Pensively.

Or so Victoria thought. Something that didn't bode well for the day ahead, if she was any judge.

She paused on that third step for a moment, wondering if she should go back to the attic room and wait for him to bellow for her. Why rush into anything? she asked herself.

But for some reason she stayed where she was, taking a good, long look at him from behind.

She wished he was short and scrawny and smelled bad as she drank in the sight of him. Or maybe fat and flabby with elephant ears and rolls of flesh rippling down his neck. Anything would be better than what he was—sculpted like an Adonis with those broad shoulders and narrow waist and that rear end that was absolute male perfection even in a pair of disreputable blue jeans that had a hole just below the right rear pocket.

Maybe she should go back upstairs, she told herself as she felt every sense kick into overdrive at just that initial view of him.

But just as she was going to retrace her path, he moved.

She thought he might have seen her and the last thing she wanted was for him to think she was cowering from him, so she nixed the idea of retreat.

"Morning," she said softly, deciding offense was the best form of defense.

Apparently he hadn't seen her, after all, because only then did he turn to acknowledge her presence. Slowly. Almost reluctantly, it seemed.

"Morning," he greeted in a toneless voice that gave no indication of his mood.

There weren't any clues in his face, either. He merely watched with a blank expression as she walked the rest of the way down the stairs.

He hadn't shaved yet and his face was shadowed in dark stubble that made him look dangerous and ruggedly handsome all at once.

It didn't help Victoria to notice that. In fact it left her all the more uneasy to realize that she, who ordinarily did not like a man with any kind of beard, let alone stubble, had butterflies in her stomach with one glance at Adam Benson's face.

And the stomach flutters only got worse when the way he was dressed threw her into a sudden flashback.

He had on a faded red Henley that she could have sworn he'd worn as a teenager. Or maybe it was just similar to a shirt from all those years ago, but the tight fit of it and the way he had the sleeves bunched up to his elbows shot her backward in time.

He also had the top button unfastened and although there hadn't been the same smattering of dark chest hair peeking through when he was younger, the whole image still brought to mind the days when he'd worked on her father's ranch and she'd sneaked peeks at him.

His jeans didn't help matters, either.

They were so threadbare there was a stringy, frayed rip at his right knee, and just above that rip was a red bandana tied around his leg.

That was what he'd done as a boy—tied a scarf like that around the lower part of his thigh. Victoria wasn't altogether sure why he did that, but she recalled him using it to wipe perspiration from his brow when he worked. It had seemed so sexy to her as a girl that it had nearly made her sweat.

In fact, it almost made her sweat now as the images of him in the past and in the present mingled in her mind. They certainly didn't help to calm those butterflies in her stomach.

"You're up early," he said amiably enough, compounding things for her when a stab of sarcasm or a critical comment or even an ominous look might have eased what had begun in her so early today.

"I guess I am," she said with a glance past him at the sun that had topped the horizon by then. "So are you, though."

"Sleeping doesn't seem to be my best thing right now."

That sounded like an admission that he was disturbed by something. A guilty conscience, maybe? Or had the kiss of the night before kept him stirred up? It definitely hadn't made for a sound night's sleep for her....

"Mountain air is supposed to have the opposite effect," she offered.

"Maybe it doesn't drift down here at the base of them and that's the problem."

Their banter was inconsequential, but what struck Victoria was that it *was* just inconsequential chitchat without any razor's edge to it, despite Adam's mood.

Had that kiss that had sent him out of the room mellowed him?

She didn't see how that was possible, but it occurred to her that maybe she shouldn't analyze it. Maybe she should just be grateful that he wasn't snapping at everything. That maybe they could even reach a kind of truce that would ease the pressure she was under.

Of course she didn't know what a truce would mean for her in terms of her attraction to him and the contrariness she counted on to keep it all under control.

But wouldn't it be nicer to not have to contend with his coldness and aloofness and arrogance and facetiousness all the time? To not have to worry that he might bite her head off at any moment?

It would be a tremendous relief, she decided.

And if it made his appeal more difficult to deal with?

She'd find a way.

"Anything in particular you'd like for breakfast?" she asked, thinking that if he could lighten up, so could she.

"How about bacon, eggs and toast?" he sug-

gested. No demand, no snide comment about her
ability to fix it.

"Coming up," she agreed, feeling genuine hope
spring to life.

"Then we can get started on the barn," he said to
her back as she headed for the kitchen.

"'We'?" she blurted before she knew she was going to.

"I thought about it and between the scraping and
the priming and the painting, it's too big a job for
one person," he answered. "And I need the exercise."

Victoria glanced over her shoulder at him. With a
body like his, exercise was the last thing he needed.

So what was the catch?

She couldn't help being suspicious.

It was one thing to hope for a kinder, gentler
Adam Benson, but for him to go so far as to work
alongside her? That didn't make sense. Especially
not when the whole point of this scheme of his was
for her to do the work.

Was he toying with her again? Just when she
thought he was going to help, would he pull out one
of his smug smiles and call her a fool? Tell her it
was her job, not his, now that their positions were
reversed?

Or was he just looking for an excuse to keep an
eye on her to make sure she did what he wanted?
That his pound of flesh truly was being exacted?

Keeping an eye on her seemed like the most likely
possibility except that he'd kept an eye on her the
day before without lifting a finger.

Or maybe the plan was to just keep her off balance with these mood swings. To leave her never knowing what he was up to.

Or maybe she was just getting paranoid.

Adam crossed the room then, set his coffee cup on the counter and actually went to the cupboard for plates, silverware and napkins to set the table.

"Is this some new twist?" Victoria asked, surprised that the words had escaped and wishing she didn't sound so wary that she gave herself away.

"'A new twist'?" he parroted.

"You being nice."

"No. No new twist.

"You're setting the table and planning to help paint the barn. That seems kind of strange."

"I told you, I need the exercise."

Victoria cast him a sideways look that conveyed even more of her disbelief.

Enough so that Adam apparently felt inclined to go on.

"Plus I want to make sure the job on the barn gets done right. And that's not going to happen unless I'm doing part of it."

Now *that* sounded more like him—a little curt, a little cutting, a little derogatory.

But only a little. Which still kept Victoria guessing.

Although even a little of his disparagement somehow reassured her that all had not changed between them overnight.

Yet as she laid strips of bacon on the griddle, that reassurance was in small quantity, too. Because she couldn't help feeling, deep down, that something *had* changed between them.

She just didn't know what it was.

As the day wore on, Victoria wasn't any more sure what was going on with Adam than she had been that morning.

The ogre she'd convinced herself he was seemed to have disappeared and left in his place someone in better spirits.

There were still moments when he threw out a comment or two that reminded her he hadn't forgiven her, but his disdain wasn't ever-present the way it had been before.

To Victoria that was a vast improvement. Not only did she not have to suffer so much of his angry disposition but he kept enough of a distance to help her gain some control over her involuntary attraction to him.

What didn't help was that she worked behind him on the barn. He went first, scraping the old paint in spots where it had blistered and peeled, and priming those areas, and she followed with the paint when the primer was dry.

The view of his backside gave her a view of the hole she'd noticed below his rear pocket that morning, and it went all the way to the skin.

The skin of the uppermost part of his thigh and the lowermost curve of his derriere.

Those brief, tiny glimpses of bare flesh, even though she tried not to look, kept the flutters in her stomach pretty consistent.

Not to mention that they kept several questions repeating themselves in her mind.

Such as, Didn't the man wear underwear?

Didn't he know the hole was back there?

How could the cool autumn day seem so hot and steamy?

Of course there were spells when she was convinced he'd worn the torn jeans just to torment her. That that was the purpose of his working on the barn with her.

But those spells were brief and she didn't actually believe that he knew what he was doing to her. Any more than she believed he had any idea that every time he untied the bandana from around his thigh, it sent her heart into palpitations to go along with the butterflies in her stomach.

Palpitations and butterflies that only got worse when he bent to replace the scarf and that hole opened up.

By the end of the afternoon, between the exertion and the excitement, Victoria felt as if she'd been through the wringer. She wondered if the more harsh comeuppance was coming from fate rather than from Adam—in the form of the simmering attraction she couldn't seem to shed no matter how hard she tried. Especially when she hadn't been able to escape Adam all day long.

They were headed inside the back door of the house when a knock on the front door picked up Adam's pace.

"Are you expecting company?" Victoria asked as

she followed behind, not happy to greet a guest in top-to-toe paint splatters.

"No one I know of," Adam answered as he opened the door.

The man who stood outside was dressed in a police uniform and he looked only slightly familiar to Victoria when she caught a glimpse of him from around Adam.

"Sloan." Adam greeted the man with surprise in his voice.

"Sorry to bother you, Adam."

Adam stepped aside and invited the officer in. Then he turned to Victoria and said, "Do you remember Sloan Ravencrest?"

Victoria knew the name more than the face or the slightly longish dark hair and darker eyes that went with it. Her folks had told her about the half Native American who was the newest sheriff's deputy. Sloan looked too young for her to have known him from school or social activities growing up.

"I do now," she said in answer to Adam's question. She offered her hand and he shook it, apologizing to her as if the first one to Adam hadn't been enough.

"I hate to barge in like this." Then, with more of his attention focused on Adam, he said, "I've been up in the mountains all day. We got a tip about Christina Montgomery being in the woods somewhere and I pulled search duty. I thought I might stop here on my way back to town and find out if you've seen anything."

"You still haven't found the mayor's daughter?" Adam asked, rather than offering any information.

The sheriff's deputy shook his head. "No, and it isn't looking good. We're leaning toward the worst case scenario."

"You think she's dead?"

Sloan shrugged, but it was clear that was just what he thought. "She's been gone awhile. Maybe an accident or foul play."

"And nothing turned up from your tip?"

"No, we didn't come across so much as a clue."

"I wish I could help you, but we've only been here since late Sunday and haven't gone farther than the barn."

Sloan Ravencrest looked slightly uncomfortable. "I know you're on your honeymoon out here."

That embarrassed Victoria. Although she couldn't be sure if it was because of what he was assuming honeymooning meant or because it didn't mean what he was assuming at all.

Adam glossed over the comment. "We haven't seen anything. And I'm sure if Sherm had, he would have said something before he left."

"Yeah, I talked to your foreman on his way through town. He couldn't tell me anything, either."

"You're welcome to stay for dinner. How about that? I'm slapping steaks under the broiler."

That was news to Victoria but she was glad to hear it. Respite from cooking was welcome as far as she was concerned.

The deputy declined. "Thanks, but I have to get back. Would you keep an eye open, though?"

"You bet. We'll be getting out into the country-side tomorrow to round up some horses. Probably camp overnight. If I see anything, I'll phone in on my cellular."

"We'd appreciate it."

Sloan turned back toward the door. But he seemed to remember Victoria at the last minute and paused to incline his head her way. "Congratulations on your marriage."

"Thanks," she answered, even though it felt very strange to accept congratulations on a sham of a marriage.

Adam exchanged a few more words with the deputy as he walked him to the door and let Sloan out.

Once he had, Victoria said, "You're cooking to-night?"

"Just the steaks. You can do the rest. But you'd better wash up first. You're a mess."

He said that last part with a hint of a smile that let her know he wasn't really insulting her.

"So are you," she countered in the same vein.

"I need to check in with my assistant. You can use the bathroom ahead of me and then get dinner started while I shower."

"Yes, Master," she said like a zombie in an old B movie, bowing at the waist and wondering at her own boldness in teasing him about his dictates.

But he didn't take offense. He merely rolled his eyes at her lame joke and headed for the telephone.

Yet the fact that he'd taken her teasing in stride also seemed like an improvement when, just twenty-four hours earlier, he would have leveled her with a withering look.

But then, twenty-four hours earlier, she wouldn't have ventured it.

Adam was on the telephone when Victoria finished showering and padded across the living room in her bathrobe to climb the stairs to the attic.

She was glad about that, not having liked the idea that his attention might be on her when her head was turbaned in a towel and she was wearing a terry-cloth robe that wasn't fit for company.

Upstairs in her small room she put on clean clothes, blow-dried her hair and then pulled the sides up in a knot at her crown, leaving the back to hang loose.

She told herself she wasn't sprucing up for Adam's sake, but just because it felt good after a day in dingy clothes and paint drippings.

She also tried to believe it.

But it wasn't easy when she ended up feeling as overlooked as a piece of furniture when Adam didn't seem to even notice her join him in the kitchen a little while later where he was seasoning the steaks. He was still talking on the phone.

Then he slipped the broiler pan into the refrigerator and took the cordless phone with him into the bathroom while Victoria went to work on the rest of their dinner.

He came out about half an hour later, freshly shaven, wearing clean clothes, and still holding the telephone to his ear.

He stayed on the phone all the while he broiled their steaks and the whole time they ate. Then, when he was finished, he moved from the table to the desk, and Victoria began to wonder if the telephone had taken root to his ear.

So much for change, Victoria thought as she cleaned the kitchen.

He finally hung up just as she closed the dishwasher.

"I'm sorry. That was just plain bad manners," he said.

Again hearing an apology from him shocked her so much she didn't know what to say.

But he didn't seem to notice that, either, as he went on. "We're in the middle of negotiations with a software company I've opted to reorganize, and apparently today was a bad day for me to be unavailable."

That seemed the perfect opportunity to finally ask about his job. "I don't know what it is you actually do for a living," she said.

Congenially enough he said, "Mergers and acquisitions is the nicest title. Corporate raider isn't as nice, but I've been called that, too."

"You take over companies?" she said as she folded the dishtowels and put them away.

"Basically. I take them over, cut the fat, sell off certain portions or break things up into parts and sell off all the parts. Whatever is the most profitable. Although some companies have enough life left in them to make it worth my while to hang on to them. It's more work restructuring and reorganizing, but in the end I'm the major stockholder in a business that can earn a higher profit than I can make from selling it off. Or, sometimes I get things in better shape, hold on for a few years and then sell when the market is better. But I didn't mean to talk on the phone all through dinner. My mother would have tanned my hide for that.''

Of course it wasn't all that big a faux pas if he were still considering Victoria the hired help. But it seemed as if she'd been elevated to a higher position than that.

Not that she was going to complain. Especially when he gave her a conciliatory smile that went a long way in warming her up.

''I think I'll go for a little walk,'' she said then, thinking only about cooling off.

''Okay. That sounds good,'' he said as if she'd invited him along.

Which she wouldn't have done because getting away from him—and from his effect on her—had been her intention. But what could she do?

''Want to get a coat?'' he asked.

Not when cooling off was her goal. ''No, I'll be fine. I'll just pull my sleeves down.''

He raised an eyebrow at that but only said, ''I think I'll grab one,'' and went into the bedroom.

When he came back he had on a black leather jacket that just skimmed his waist and looked buttery soft and terrific on him.

It didn't help Victoria's cause one wit as she drank in the sight of him and felt every sense stand up to take notice. But all she could do was try to not pay attention to how great he looked and head for the front door with Adam following behind.

The night air was cooler than Victoria had anticipated and she immediately regretted not bringing a coat. But she wouldn't admit it, telling herself the chill was therapeutic. Like a cold shower.

She left the porch at a brisk pace to generate some internal heat and headed toward the lake. It stood calm and shadowed by the huge elm tree that hovered over it and it seemed so serene she hoped she might find some serenity of her own just by circling it.

For Adam, her brisk pace was more of a leisurely stroll because his legs were much longer. He fell in beside her without a problem.

"So tell me how you got to be where you are today," she suggested as they walked.

"You mean, how did I get into the business I'm in?"

"Yeah."

"I started out as an investment counselor and stockbroker. That gave me contact with some wealthy people and a finger on the pulse of what was going on in some viable companies that weren't doing well. I could see where there was money to be made in taking them over. I saved everything I could of my own money, raised the rest from investors willing to take a risk, and one thing led to another."

"I never knew you were interested in the financial world."

"There's a lot you didn't know about me."

"But it's a long way from working on a ranch to Wall Street."

"I worked on the Chicago Stock Exchange, not Wall Street."

"Still."

"I liked the ranch work. The animals. The outdoors. The wide-open spaces. But I wanted to make money, be my own boss, and following in my father's footsteps wasn't going to get me that. After we left Whitehorn I went to four different high schools before I graduated—that was how many towns we moved to that year. I wasn't going to be a vagabond, either, so I did my damnedest to get a scholarship to college, which I did. I still had to work so I could send money to my mother to help ends meet, but scholarships paid my way through school. I got a business degree, then an M.B.A. Then I went to work."

He said that with enough inflection to let her know he hadn't just earned his degrees and then gotten a job. She could tell he'd gone after success with a vengeance.

"You were determined to make something of yourself," she said as they reached the far side of the lake. As she spoke, her teeth chattered suddenly, letting him know just how cold she was.

He took off the leather jacket and slipped it around her shoulders.

"Here, I've been warm for the first half of the walk, you can be warm for the second."

"No, that's okay," she protested. But there wasn't much strength behind it. Particularly when his hands lingered at her shoulders for longer than they needed to and the heat of his body encased her every bit as much as the soft leather. When the scent of his aftershave rose from the collar of the coat, it all combined to make her light-headed.

Then he took his hands away, shoving them into his pockets as if they were safer there, and addressed her comment instead. "Yes, I was determined to make something of myself. Thanks in no small part to what happened that night in your father's barn. And to my family afterward," he admitted grudgingly.

"So it wasn't *all* bad?" she ventured hopefully.

"It was all bad. But something good came out of it," he qualified, obviously still not ready to let her off the hook.

Which made it seem like a good time to change the subject.

"We're rounding up horses tomorrow?" she asked.

"First you get to clean the stable," he informed her with an edge to his voice that said it was just what she deserved and she shouldn't forget it. "Then we'll head out. There are four prime breeders that I've had pastured at the farthest corner of the ranch for the summer. They need to be brought in before it gets much colder or heavy snowfall hits. But since we won't leave until the afternoon, we'll just reach them by dark. We'll camp overnight and head back the next morning."

"Why not just wait and leave early the next morning so we can get back the same night?"

"And miss making you rough it?"

"Ah," she said, a little slow on the uptake. "More of my comeuppance—a night on the range like a ranch hand."

He just glanced over at her and smiled a satisfied smile that let her know she was finally with the program.

Then he said, "Just make sure you pack warm enough clothes and a coat."

It might be worth it not to so she could borrow his, she thought as she hugged the leather jacket around her and snuggled deep inside it.

Neither of them said much of anything else through the rest of the walk. Only the chirp of autumn crickets serenaded them.

But it was a soothing sound that seemed to emphasize that they were alone. Together. And even though Victoria tried not to admit to herself that she liked it, she did.

They approached the house again and before Victoria knew it they were climbing the steps that led to the porch. Something about that made it seem very much as if he'd just walked her home.

"Well, thank you for a lovely evening," she joked, in keeping with that.

Adam picked up on her joke. When they reached the front door he acted as if he didn't have the right to go in.

"We'll have to do it again sometime," he said, playing along.

"That would be nice, but I'm being kept awfully busy."

They'd left the door open and the light coming through the screen door cast a golden glow on him as Victoria looked up into his amused and terribly handsome face.

"Are you trying to give me the brush-off here?" he asked, sounding much the way he had when they'd flirted as teens.

"The brush-off? You?" she answered in mock disbelief. "Why would I do that?"

"I've been asking myself that same question for years now."

"I'd have to be crazy. Or a huge coward."

One well-shaped eyebrow rose. "Which is it?"

She pretended to think about it. "Both. But I'm not proud of either."

He nodded his head and she had the sense that he was closer to accepting this banter as an apology than he had been to accepting the one she'd delivered their first night there. The one she'd given in all seriousness.

Their gazes seemed to lock then and Victoria searched his pewter-gray eyes.

Maybe for forgiveness.

Maybe for something more.

Maybe for a sign that somewhere beneath it all he might still have a trace of the warmer feelings for her that he'd had all those years ago.

And at that moment she knew that the reason for going along with his marriage ultimatum hadn't only been to help her parents.

There was a tiny, secret part of her that also wanted him to feel the way he had before. A part of her that wanted to know if she could reach him the way she had then. If she could wipe away the damage she'd done. And maybe start over again....

He seemed to be looking for something, too. His eyes delved deeply into hers, penetrating them, holding them. Then she saw his brows take an almost imperceptible dip together just before he leaned in and kissed her.

Not a kiss like the previous night, which had almost been like a schoolboy snatching a smooch on a dare.

This was a real kiss with lips that were smooth, and parted only slightly, and unhurried.

Lips she couldn't help responding to. Answering. Letting them have their way with her own mouth....

But then it was over. Maybe not as quickly or as frantically as the kiss the evening before, but still much too soon.

Much, much too soon.

Victoria was almost afraid to open her eyes. Afraid she'd find the same look of self-disgust in Adam's features. The same look of abhorrence. The same drive to get away from her, as if she were the devil incarnate tempting him to evil.

But she couldn't just stand there with her eyes closed forever.

She had to face the music if there was music to face.

When she finally cast a glance up at him she didn't find any of what had been there the previous night. Instead she found him staring down at her quizzically.

For only a moment, though. Then he opened the screen and swept an arm in front of him to let her know he was holding it for her, as if they were still playing the game that had started when they'd reached the porch.

Victoria went inside, holding his coat closed around herself as if it were his arms. Arms that hadn't reached out to take her into them when he'd kissed her. Arms her body had a powerful yen to feel.

But when she turned, expecting to see that he'd followed her inside, she discovered him standing on the other side of the closed screen door, as if he really had brought her home from a date and wasn't coming in.

"Another early morning tomorrow," was all he said. "See you then."

There was nothing antagonistic in his words or in his tone. It was a simple statement. A simple goodnight.

From outside looking in.

Victoria wondered if it was just in keeping with the game, or if he was reminding himself of how things had been twenty years earlier—her in one place, him only an observer from afar.

If that was the case, she couldn't feel much hope for a fresh start.

Except that there was still that kiss lingering on her lips and helping to strike a tiny ember of hope, anyway.

"'Night," she said quietly, slipping out of his coat and laying it lovingly over the back of the sofa before she climbed the stairs to the attic room, taking confusion to bed with her.

Confusion about him.

Confusion about herself and her own feelings, too.

Five

Victoria placed a call to her mother first thing the next morning just to check in. She pretended that packing up the ranch was going well and then learned that her father was having less trouble sleeping before ending the call to take on the day. Mucking out a barn wasn't something Victoria had ever had to do as the daughter of Charles Rutherford.

But it wasn't so bad, she thought as she did the chore after Adam repeated the order—the only thing he'd said to her before she'd left the cabin.

Of course the job was less trouble than it might have been. It helped that no animals had been housed in the stable for the summer, and mice and vermin hadn't yet found their way inside to get out of the cold. Mainly she just had a whole lot of sweeping to do before she hosed out troughs and stalls and then the floor.

The good thing about it was that Adam hadn't opted to help, so she had time to think without him as a distraction.

Time to remind herself that she shouldn't be giving in to her attraction to him. To her feelings for him.

Because, yes, she did have feelings for him.

Much as she didn't want to. Much as she didn't understand exactly what those feelings were.

And in spite of the fact that she'd tried to keep herself from having any feelings toward him at all.

There were just so many things going on with her.

There were the remnants of the crush she'd had on him as a girl. They cropped up at the oddest moments, in flashbacks so vivid it seemed as if she were right back on her father's ranch, the belle of the ball, unable to keep her mind off the help.

There was the part of her that still couldn't keep her mind off Adam. Or her eyes. The part that feasted on every glimpse of him. That put him in her thoughts day and night. That made everything inside her come to life whenever he walked into the room.

And then there was a part of her that wanted to make up to him the wrong she'd done so long ago.

That was the part that worried her.

She wanted so badly to make amends for what she'd done that she was willing to overlook some of the negative things he dished out. She turned the other cheek when, never in her life, had she allowed anyone to treat her the way he did when he wasn't being civil. Never in her life had she complied so docilely with gruff orders. Never in her life had she ignored snide comments about herself or her abilities.

Yet she was accepting it all from him because she considered it part of those amends she was making.

What if, on the flip side of that, she was viewing any crumb of kindness or pleasantry as a banquet? What if she was reading more than she should into those moments when he treated her less harshly?

What if her reaction to them was just as out of proportion?

Such as when she melted the minute he turned the heat of his eyes on her. Or when she got weak-kneed at nothing more than the sight or smell of him. And then there was the fact that she actually had feelings that came to life when all he was offering was common courtesy.

Was she that desperate?

She didn't know. She wished she had answers to her own questions, but she didn't.

"The whole thing is just too confusing," she said out loud in the empty stable as she swept with more fury.

She was married to a man who resented her on one level and seemed to be attracted to her on another.

She was attracted to him and leery of him at the same time.

She felt as if she almost deserved some of his bad attitude toward her. And then she was walking on cloud nine anytime he smiled at her.

Plus, she seemed incapable of controlling her own impulses just because he pressed his lips to hers.

There was something off kilter about this whole thing.

Something definitely off kilter about two short, silly little kisses knocking her socks off and leaving her dazed and churned up inside and wanting to melt into arms that hadn't even wrapped around her. She'd been so starved for more that she had actually gone to bed both of the two previous nights listening, hoping for sounds of Adam climbing the stairs to the attic. She imagined what it would be like for him to come to her room wearing nothing but his jeans, with that glorious chest bare. He'd sit on the edge of her bed and bend to kiss her again, longer, deeper, holding her so close to him her breasts would be flattened against his hard, hot chest. His hands would roam—

Oh, no, she was doing it again—somehow going from merely thinking about him to losing herself in a fantasy.

"See," she said as if she'd just proved her point to someone else.

It was crazy that so little could lead to so much.

But it kept happening. Again and again.

Just the way it had when she was a girl.

But she wasn't a girl anymore. She was a grown woman. A grown woman who shouldn't have been so overly susceptible to any man, regardless of what misdeed she might have committed against him.

She just didn't understand why it was happening now. In the worst of circumstances. When she knew better. When she was trying to not let it happen.

Confusing. The whole thing was just so confusing.

As she dragged the hose into the barn she told herself all over again that she had to protect herself. The only way to do that was to not give in to this weakness she seemed to have for him. To not give in to the feelings for him. The fantasies of him. The desires and cravings for him.

She couldn't trust where they were coming from. She couldn't trust herself. And she certainly couldn't trust Adam. Or his intentions. Or where this all might lead.

It just wasn't a time to be falling for the guy.

Okay, so it made her life more pleasant when he was being nice, when they could talk or work side by side or share a meal or take a walk.

But that didn't mean she had to end up kissing him. Or let a simple kiss or the sight of him or thought of him catapult her into so much more. Even if it was only in her mind.

Although the desires and cravings were in her body, too.

The fact was, she was getting carried away, and that was never smart.

Especially when this was not a normal situation.

She had to remember that. And she had to keep in mind that it was possible that none of her feelings were normal, either. They were a combination of the past, of being under whatever his current influence was, of reality and fantasy, all tangled up together.

Nothing good was likely to come out of that tangle.

"So quit taking chances," she ordered herself.

Because that was what she was doing—taking a huge risk every time she let her guard drop. Every time she gave in to enjoying being with him or let her mind fill with images of him. Every time she let him kiss her or kissed him back.

It had to stop.

The trouble was, even though she was determined to keep her perspective, she knew that it was the most difficult thing she'd ever had to do.

So far, she hadn't been able to do it, despite her best intentions.

"But that doesn't mean you can't start today," she told herself, sounding like a motivational speaker.

She just had to quit hanging on his every word, his every nuance.

She just had to quit noticing every detail about him.

She just had to quit letting him get to her.

Victoria turned on the nozzle to the hose full-blast and braced herself against the jolt as a forceful spray shot out.

In her mind she pictured herself bracing against the power of Adam. Keeping him and his effect on her at bay.

From now on she was going to put whatever she had into resisting him.

Making amends was one thing, but letting him into her heart was something else again.

She wasn't going to let it happen.

She really, really wasn't.

Victoria and Adam headed out on horseback that afternoon. Adam was still barely speaking to her, giving orders but not much more. And once he'd mounted his big black stallion, he'd set off without waiting for her, leaving her to ride several yards behind him.

She could have caught up—her chestnut mare was young and energetic—but she chose not to. What was the point when he was ignoring her, anyway?

Not that she understood why he'd been more mellow the day after the first kiss but back to sullen and aloof the day after the second. But since his stand-offishness aided her most recent plans to keep her own distance, she just decided to let him be and enjoy the ride.

It had been a long time since she'd been up on a horse. Even visits home to her folks on the ranch hadn't occasioned many horseback rides.

But the mare was gentle and Victoria got the feel for it again before long, leaving her free to concentrate on the scenery.

Because the mountains were so nearby, the ground they traveled was anything but flat. Hills large and small rose up to be climbed and then dipped into valleys where the grass was still fairly green even if the wildflowers had gone out of bloom.

The closer they got to the mountains the bigger the hills that would eventually become the taller, jagged peaks of the Crazy Mountains. The sky was a crystal-clear blue, the sun was high and had lost its blistering heat, a slight autumn breeze brought with it the scent of fresh pine and spruce, and if Victoria had to be sentenced to roughing it, she couldn't have asked for a better day.

Of course not every glance took in only nature's splendor. A fair share of them fell on Adam up ahead of her.

No one would guess from looking at him that he was anything but a cowboy today.

The jeans he had on underneath his old leather chaps were saddle-worn. His chambray shirt looked as if it had seen any number of cattle drives, as did the leather vest he wore over it and the sturdy brown cowboy boots that were wedged into the stirrups. He even had a sweat-stained Stetson atop his head and Victoria had never seen anyone who sat a horse better than he did—tall, straight-backed, so easy in the saddle it was as if he and the horse were one.

It was something to see.

But she fought the urge to simply watch him ride, determined not to succumb to that temptation and where she knew it would take her.

As afternoon turned into early evening, they reached the pasture where Adam's four horses had spent the summer. There were fences far off in the distance, but for the most part it was a wide-open space at the very foot of the mountains.

All four horses were Thoroughbred stallions. Two Victoria guessed to be not much more than two-year-olds and still had some immaturity to them. One was a beautiful blood bay and the other a sorrel.

Their companions were both a liver-chestnut color and had clearly reached full growth at probably fifteen to sixteen hands each. It didn't take a horse expert to see that what Adam had out there was prime stock that would earn him a pretty penny in stud fees.

He reined his horse to a stop under a stand of three oaks whose leaves were turning gold and bronze and just beginning to fall into the stream that ran several feet to the north of them.

Victoria pulled up next to him.

"You can make camp here under the trees, while I get the horses haltered and tethered for the night.

That way we can break camp first thing in the morning and be able to head home without having to catch them then.''

A bit of pique over his previous silence caused her to say, ''You mean I'm not assigned both chores?''

He arched an eyebrow at her cheeky tone. ''As if you know how to do either,'' he said sarcastically.

''I was raised on a ranch, you know,'' she countered the same way. She didn't know why she was pushing this but apparently something about his switch in attitudes again had set her off and she couldn't seem to stop herself.

''You were raised on a ranch all right. But you never got your hands dirty. I was there to see it, remember?''

Every word out of his mouth only seemed to increase her indignation and determination to prove to him that she hadn't been merely a spoiled little rich girl. Even though that was actually what she had been.

''I'll get the horses *and* make camp,'' she heard herself say, thinking even as she did that maybe she'd gone a little crazy.

His arched eyebrow went higher still. ''Is that so?''

''And I don't want you to lift a finger. Not a single finger. No matter what,'' her bluster continued, ignoring the little voice in the back of her mind that reminded her that she hadn't a clue how to either build a campsite or gather the horses.

''Careful or I might take you at your word,'' he warned.

"I expect you to."

He sighed and shook his head. "You can't do it," he said fatalistically but without any challenge in his voice.

Which only added fuel to the fire of her foolish temper.

"I *can* do it and I *will* do it, and don't you dare butt in."

Oh dear, she really had gone out of her mind.

He chuckled slightly, closed his eyes and scratched the highest curve of his cheekbone with one index finger. Then he opened his eyes again and looked at her with pure amusement. "Okay," he finally conceded. "I'll just sit and watch unless you ask for my help."

"Don't hold your breath."

He just smiled a small smile that said she'd made things more interesting for him. And that he knew it was only a matter of time before she admitted defeat.

It made Victoria all the more determined. Even as she realized she'd gotten herself into somewhat of a pickle.

Despite the fact that she'd grown up on a ranch it hadn't taught her much about what to do with the animals. As far as she'd been concerned, when she'd wanted to ride a horse she'd gone out to the barn, told one of the ranch hands and they'd saddled and bridled the animal of her choice and then led it to her. When she was finished riding she'd handed the reins over to someone else who had taken care of whatever needed to be done.

She had no idea what to expect of these four

horses she was now supposed to catch—or how to go about that.

"Are they trained?" she asked, hoping to finesse some information out of Adam.

"Yep."

So much for that.

"Will they come if I whistle for them?"

That made him smile bigger. "You can try," he said as if he knew it wouldn't work but he'd get a kick out of seeing it.

Since Victoria didn't trust him, she made a circle out of her thumb and index finger, put them between pursed lips and let out an ear-splitting whistle.

The blood bay raised his head but none of the others paid any attention at all. And not one of them took so much as a step.

Adam seemed to enjoy it, though. "They'll likely be rusty and a little wild after being left on their own all this time. It'll take some reminding of their training before they're back up to speed," he said, almost as if the whistle might have otherwise worked.

"What should I do, whisper in their ears what they're supposed to do?"

"Takes more than that."

But still he didn't give her any more help than that. Just as she'd ordered.

"Will I be able to ride up to them, slip the halters on and lead them back here?" She tried again.

Adam shrugged, taking her too much at her word—damn him anyway. "See where it gets you. You never know," he said casually enough.

"Is there a better way?" she demanded.

"Do you want me to do this?" he asked as if she might be ready to give up before she'd even begun.

"No. I don't want you to do this," her silly bluster made her say. "I was just trying to save time by getting your opinion."

She could tell he saw through her but all he said was, "You can try luring them with some grain."

Adam dismounted then, letting the reins of his own horse fall forward before he added, "You'll find a sack of it in your saddlebag."

Adam had done the packing of both horses, tying bedrolls behind the saddles and stuffing the saddlebags with whatever else was needed, so Victoria had no idea what they'd brought with them beyond her own few personal items. She took his word for the fact that there was a sack of grain in one of hers.

"Shall I stay in the saddle or get down on foot?" she asked.

"I'd ride out a little closer then get down on foot. If your own horse is nearby it'll save you walking the whole way back, but if you ride right up to them they'll likely shy away. But the first thing I'd do is string a tether line between those two trees over there so you have something to tie them to when you do get a hold of them." Then he added with another amused smile, "That's just me, though. Feel free to do it your own way."

He was enjoying this, Victoria realized. But she tried to ignore it.

"What if I don't tie a rope to tether them to first?" she asked out of pure contrariness.

"If you don't, you won't have anything to tie them to when you get them back here, will you?"

Good point.

Since there was a coil of rope hanging from her saddle, she got down off her horse and took the rope to tie around one tree trunk, stretching it to another to tie the other end around that one. Although neither knot was fancy, when she stood back to assess her handiwork, she judged them adequate.

Adam took four leather halters from his saddle and held them out to her. "Looks like you're ready. If you still think you want to take this on, that is."

That came out dubiously, as if he didn't think her knot-tying was quite as adequate as she did.

Or maybe he was just trying to rattle her. She decided not to let him. "Just sit back and watch me."

She took the halters, got back on her horse and headed toward the other end of the pasture.

When she was several feet away from the horses she dismounted, slung two of the halters over her shoulder, searched her saddlebags for the sack of grain, and turned toward her quarry.

With a handful of grain in her palm and the rest of the sack stuffed in the pocket of her jeans, she said, "Hi, boys," in a gentle, soft voice, heading toward one of the older stallions who was nearest.

He watched her coming, seemingly curious about her and what she was offering him, but stayed where he was.

"Good boy," she cooed. "Bet you haven't had a treat all summer, have you? This'll taste better than grass for a change."

The horse let her come close so he could nibble the grain from her hand and once he had, Victoria tried to slip the halter over his head.

But just as she thought she was going to get it there, he caught it in his mouth.

A bridle had a mouthpiece and was meant to be used when a horse was ridden. But for merely leading the animal, a halter was used, and it wasn't supposed to go in the horse's mouth.

But now that the stallion had it there, he'd clenched his teeth around it and wouldn't let go.

"Come on," she cajoled, tugging it.

It didn't budge.

"Having trouble out there?"

Adam's voice wasn't loud across the distance and Victoria decided to pretend she hadn't heard him.

Again she tried to get the horse to release the halter by tapping lightly on his nose. But he ignored her as effectively as she was ignoring Adam.

She was about at her wit's end when she remembered the grain and reached into the sack for more, coaxing the horse into finally opening his mouth so she could release the halter and get it properly over his head.

"I won't make that mistake again," she confided to the stallion as she fastened the halter.

Taking the first horse with her, she approached the second the same way—grain in her palm, speaking softly to him.

The technique worked again and, true to her word, she was careful when she slipped the halter on, not giving the second horse a chance to get it in his mouth.

Before she knew it she was back on her own horse and leading the two older of the stallions to her tether line.

So there, Benson! she thought, still paying him no outward attention whatsoever even though she was dying to cast him a smile as smug as those he so frequently threw her way.

"Two down, two to go," he said from where he sat with his back against one of the trees, his legs bent at the knees and spread wide apart, his wrists resting on them, his hands dangling.

Victoria didn't honor his comment but just remounted and headed back for the other horses, confident that she wouldn't have any more trouble with the two younger stallions than she'd had with the older.

Unfortunately her confidence was unwarranted.

The two younger horses seemed to find her as amusing as Adam did.

She proceeded exactly the way she had with the other animals, but these two were less interested in the proffered grain than they were in toying with her.

They let her get close, then dipped their heads and darted away with a snort that sounded very much like a horse version of a laugh.

Victoria tried to have patience, but when this went on for a good half hour, patience got less and less easy to come by.

"Could you give me a break, boys?" she finally said.

That perked up the ears on the blood bay so she went on talking to it as she slowly, very slowly, approached yet again.

"I'm in a bind here. See that guy sitting under the tree over there? Well, he'd like it if I'd go whining to him that I can't do this. But I'm not going to give him that satisfaction. So we could be at this all night, but sooner or later you'll have to give in because I won't have it any other way."

And with that she got the halter over the horse's head and felt a huge surge of relief.

Three down, one to go.

She tried the monologue with the remaining animal, but he was less sympathetic. The blood bay wasn't helping matters. Every time Victoria got close enough to lunge for the sorrel, the blood bay pulled the other way. The elusive sorrel dodged out of reach and she ended up grasping thin air over and over again.

To make matters worse, she caught sight of Adam and could tell even from that distance that he was grinning at the spectacle she was making.

"Have you boys ever heard of the glue factory?" she asked her mischievous charges.

But the threat didn't do her any more good than anything else had and it took her another half hour of trial and error before she finally haltered the last horse, too.

Regardless of how long it had taken, she was feeling pretty pleased with herself as she walked the animals back to where her own horse was waiting. She never expected the two horses to team up against her.

The sorrel abruptly veered in front of her, just as the blood bay, in mulish stubbornness, came to a sharp stop then dug in his heels and pulled her backward.

Down she went, landing on her posterior and being dragged just enough to cost her her grip of both lead straps so the two animals could merrily trot out of reach once more.

The sound of Adam's roaring laughter echoed through the canyon, dwindling only as he rode the big black stallion to where she was just getting to her feet.

"You all right?" he asked, barely suppressing the humor in his voice.

"Just dandy," she answered curtly since only her pride was injured.

"Guess I'd better take over from here if I ever want to get this done tonight. Do you still want to try setting up camp or do I need to do that, too?"

"I can do both," she went on insisting despite the evidence to the contrary.

"Just set up camp," Adam said decisively.

Then he pulled his rope from his saddle, formed it into a lasso and trotted off to rope the ornery horses before Victoria even had time to get to her mare.

"I'd brush off some of that dirt on your backside if I were you," he suggested as he rode past her, leading the blood bay and the sorrel behind him.

Victoria muttered the whole way back to the trees about arrogant showoffs who got their jollies at other people's expense.

She stopped muttering as she joined Adam at the

trees and instead said, "So what do I do to set up camp?" You big jerk, she added in her head.

"You'll need wood to burn and rocks to put around it to keep the fire from spreading. You can fill the coffeepot with water from that stream over there—it has been tested and it's drinkable—and then lay out the sleeping bags while I fix dinner."

"You're fixing dinner?" she said with far more surprise and sarcasm in her tone than she'd used the previous night when he'd broiled steaks.

"I didn't bring enough food to take the risk of you burning it," he informed congenially.

Victoria bit back a nasty retort because she knew that if she let herself get started telling him what she thought of him she might never stop.

Instead she simply went to work, heading in the direction of the stream and the stones that lined its banks.

When she'd gathered everything she went to work building a fire. It took her several tries but by the time night settled over them she had a pretty decent blaze going.

As she laid out both bedrolls—at exact opposite sides of the fire—Adam emptied cans of chili and beans into an iron frying pan he held over the flames.

When the chili and beans were warm he ladled them onto tin plates, handed Victoria one and sat across the fire from her to eat.

He wore a smile on his face, as if he were replaying her mishap with the horses in his mind's eye and enjoying it as much as the first time.

Obviously whatever demons he'd brought with

him to breakfast that morning had been dispelled. Or passed on to Victoria.

"I'm so glad I can provide you with comic relief," she heard herself say before she'd weighed the wisdom of it.

"Me, too," he agreed.

"I think the level you've sunk to today is uncalled for."

"Do you now. Why is that?"

"You seem to delight in humiliating me."

"If you'll recall it was your idea to go after the horses, not mine. Seems to me that makes it you humiliating yourself. I was just lucky enough to be your audience."

"Lucky enough? Luck has nothing to do with my being in this whole situation. It's all by your design."

"If you hadn't spent so many years as the pampered pet, you'd know how to do a thing or two. Maybe you should think of this as a belated education."

"Kind of like throwing someone who doesn't know how to swim into a lake," she said facetiously. "And you're sadistic enough to laugh if it looks like they might drown."

"I don't think I'd call what's going on here sadism."

"What would you call it? Oh, wait, I know—comeuppance."

"First of all let me remind you—again—that what you just did was your own choice and it was *you* who told *me* to sit back and watch. But over and above that, what I'd call it is the same kind of thing that went on at that slumber party you had the last summer I was on your father's ranch. The one when you had your old man get me out of bed to dive after Bridget Moss's heirloom ring that you all claimed she'd lost in the pool when you were swimming. As I recall I spent an hour at that while you and your girlfriends sat on the patio watching and giggling as if I was a sideshow monkey giving you all a private performance. And then didn't Bridget Moss just happen to find the ring in her pocket, after all. Surprise, surprise! Now *that* was uncalled for.''

''Okay, fine. Guilty as charged. I was a despicable little creep as a teenager—''

''At my expense,'' he said, echoing her earlier thoughts about his amusement at hers.

''At your expense—'' she confirmed, having her words cut off again when he went on.

''With no thought whatsoever to my feelings or to how you might be embarrassing me or to what even worse consequences could come out of those games you played with me.''

''Yes, all of it. Every bit of it,'' she shouted at him. ''I regret it. I'm sorry. And I'm here trying to make up for it. As far as I'm concerned what I did as a kid may have been horrible and hurtful and self-ish and cowardly and snobbish, but I was a kid. What *you* are is a vindictive man who can't seem to let go of any slight that was ever committed against you. Well, fine. You want me to jump through hoops and embarrass myself and work my tail off and take all the venom you've saved up for twenty years, that's what I'm here to do. But the truth is that you don't even know what you want from me.

"One minute you're cracking the whip, the next minute you're working by my side, the minute after that you're flirting with me and then you're punishing me for that. Except for the times when you're coming on to me and then leaving me hanging to prove how mean and rotten it is to lead someone on. So okay, you want your pound of flesh? I'm giving you your pound of flesh. But let's keep this where it belongs. You hate me, you want me to suffer the way you suffered, you want to get back at me for everything I ever did to you, knowingly or not. But in the meantime, keep your distance from me because you're so successful at your revenge that I'm beginning to hate you right back. Congratulations!"

Okay, so maybe she should have stuck to her previous policy of keeping her mouth shut. Because she'd been right—once she'd gotten started she'd also gotten carried away.

But at that moment she didn't care. In fact, she could have said even more now that she was on a roll.

She didn't, though.

Instead she took her eating utensils, stood and marched to the stream to wash them off, still fuming but in more control of herself as she began to think about the swimming pool incident he'd brought up.

She remembered it well. But she hadn't been at fault for that. Bridget Moss had claimed she'd lost the ring and put up such a fuss that Victoria had been forced to ask her father to get someone to go into the pool, to look for it.

Bridget had suggested Adam. She'd said that she'd seen him go into the caretaker's house that he and his family lived in only moments before, so she knew he was awake and couldn't Mr. Rutherford please, please, please ask him to see if he could find her ring.

So, all right, yes, the eleven teenage girls had all sat on the patio watching Adam dive for the ring. And yes, there had been giggling. But no one had been making fun of him.

On the contrary, those giggles were over the fact that he'd looked so incredibly good in nothing but his swimming trunks.

Every time he'd come up for air, that gloriously handsome face had broken the surface with water streaming off him, his broad chest rising into view, thick arms reaching up so massive hands could wipe the moisture out of his eyes and slick back hair that had been longer then.

Victoria remembered that image vividly. The sharp vee of his torso. The muscles of his back swelling behind his ribcage. His biceps as defined as if they'd been carved from stone. The strong column of his neck. The narrowness of his waist. The line of hair that went from his navel to disappear into trunks that hadn't left a whole lot to the imagination—

She was doing it again, she realized suddenly. She was letting her mind wander to mental pictures of Adam that did intolerable things to her insides. Even when she was furious with him.

But the point was, she reminded herself as she tried to get her head of steam back, she had not purposely set him up for that incident all those years ago. And she certainly hadn't been making fun of him.

She'd been jealous that her friends were getting a glimpse of what she'd been secretly spying on all summer and didn't want to share.

Adam appeared out of the darkness just then, hunkering down beside the stream to perform the same chore with his own plate, silverware and the frying pan.

"Feel better?" he asked without a bit of remorse but with a whole lot of condescension.

Victoria considered pushing him into the stream, but she didn't. She also didn't answer him. If he could give her the silent treatment when it suited him, she could give him the silent treatment when it suited her.

She shook the water off her plate, letting droplets fly every which way, including at Adam, and then she returned to the campsite to take off her shoes and crawl into her sleeping bag.

The sooner this day was over, the better.

Besides, it was getting very cold. But when she tried to zip the sleeping bag, the zipper got stuck about midway up the side.

She didn't know much about camping but she could tell just from the cold air seeping into the downy interior of the bedroll that her only chance of keeping warm throughout the night was to have the thing zipped all the way.

She sat up to assess what the problem was, thinking she'd probably caught some of the flannel lining. But there wasn't anything stuck in the zipper's teeth. It was just much like the stallion that had clamped his jaws around the halter earlier and refused to let go. She couldn't make the thing budge.

"Need some help?" Adam asked sardonically as he walked by on his return from the stream.

Again, Victoria didn't answer. She just went on tugging at the zipper, trying to move it in either direction and failing.

She didn't think she could find her way back to Adam's ranch in the dark or at that moment she would have gotten up, saddled the mare and ridden out of there as fast as she could. She was just so angry. So frustrated. So irritated.

A small, high-pitched shriek escaped her throat as she put everything she had into forcing the zipper.

But it still didn't move.

"Lie back."

The order came from overhead before Victoria realized Adam had retraced his steps around the fire from his own sleeping bag to stand beside her.

"Just go away," she said through gritted teeth.

"Lie back," he repeated in a tone that held as much threat as command.

She decided that, rather than argue, it was quicker and easier to do what he said, hope he could get the zipper up and that then he'd leave her alone.

So she laid back.

He knelt down next to her without another word and went to work on the stuck zipper.

Victoria tried not to look at him, staring up at the sky through the canopy of tree branches. But somehow she couldn't keep her gaze there. It went all on its own to Adam.

The fire glow gilded his face, no longer amused or even complacent-looking. He was frowning again, and too deeply for it to be merely due to the problem with her zipper.

Yet he was still so astonishingly handsome, he almost didn't seem real.

He finally got the zipper to move, sliding it closed then open again past the spot where it had stuck.

With that accomplished he said, "Lift your head," and reached for her saddle where she'd put it beside the sleeping bag. "Lift your head," he repeated when curiosity kept her from doing it immediately.

Victoria lifted her head and he put the saddle beneath it, like a pillow.

It did make her more comfortable but she couldn't bring herself to thank him.

Maybe he was waiting for her to, though, since even after he'd done that he didn't move.

Instead he stayed there, looming over her with one hand on the ground on either side of her shoulders as if he were going to do a push-up over her.

"You're wrong, you know," he said then in a low, solemn voice that sounded as if he were confiding something in her. "I don't want you to hate me."

Victoria still didn't say anything. She just went on watching him so close above her.

"And my real problem," he continued, "is that I don't hate you anymore, either."

She raised her chin and had just begun to open her mouth to ask how that could be when he kissed her. A kiss that seemed to claim her, that seemed driven to claim her.

A kiss that went rapidly from almost being fierce to more tender. More engaging. More enticing. More intriguing.

At first Victoria was going to pull her hands out of the sleeping bag, turn her head and push him away. But somehow that wasn't what she did.

She kissed him back.

Initially just as fiercely as he kissed her. Then just as tenderly.

Before she knew it, she was lost in that kiss more than either of the two that had preceded it. Lost in warm lips that opened over hers. Lost in expertise that urged her to relax, to savor that moment and that kiss and the tiny charges of light that were going off inside her in response.

His hands found their way underneath her, underneath even the sleeping bag, pulling her up only enough so that her spine arched and her breasts pressed against his chest as her head fell further back, letting him deepen the kiss even more.

Out came her arms from the bedroll, though not to push him away. They snaked around him until she could fill her palms with the hardness of his back, powerful even through leather and chambray, holding him as tightly as he held her.

A part of Victoria knew she'd lost her mind to be doing this. Worse than doing it, enjoying it. Reveling in the feel of his mouth over hers, his arms around her, her arms around him. But that didn't seem to be the part that mattered at that moment.

The only thing that mattered was that she was there, being soundly, resoundingly kissed by him. The way she'd longed to be both times before, with mouths suddenly open and tongues getting to know each other in torrid abandon that brought things to life within her. Things that had long lain dormant. Things that cried out for fewer barriers between them. Things that shrieked for the feel of flesh against flesh. Things that wiped away all other thoughts and left her straining to be even closer to him....

But then he ended the kiss.

He lay her back down with as much care as if she were made of china.

He didn't leave even then, though. He searched her eyes with his and there was a look of disbelief in them before he shook his head.

"No, I definitely don't want you to hate me. Damn it all to hell," he said almost more to himself than to her.

Then he got up and walked in the direction of the stream again, disappearing into the darkness.

There was only one thing that was certain in Victoria's mind: this whole thing was insane, including maybe Adam.

But she was no better. Because as mad as she'd been at him, as mad as part of her still was, there was also that part of her—the same part that had responded to his kiss—that wished he would come back and join her in her sleeping bag to make love to her right out there under the stars.

The way she'd dreamed of since she was a girl.

A dream that no amount of anger or frustration or irritation or annoyance seemed able to wipe away.

Six

Adam didn't say more than six sentences to Victoria all day Thursday. He had her break camp just after dawn and each of them led two horses back home. She brushed down all four stallions and got them settled in, while he spent the remainder of the day and into the evening on the telephone and at the computer and fax machine conducting business.

He managed to not succumb to the urge to talk to her once he finally finished work, the way he had every other night they'd been at the ranch.

And he resisted the even stronger urge to repeat any of those three kisses they'd shared in evenings past—something he considered quite a feat.

But by Friday he didn't feel any better than he had since their argument Wednesday night.

Of course it didn't brighten his spirits that Victoria wasn't speaking to him, either, except out of necessity. But still the things she'd said to him in the heat of anger kept gnawing at him and by Friday when he decided the chore of the day would be for her to repair the cabin roof, he also decided that some hard physical labor might help clear his own head.

The trouble was, once they'd both climbed the ladder and gone to work pounding nails through loose shingles into the rooftop, each beat of the hammer seemed to echo Victoria's last words when she'd told him off Wednesday night.

I'm beginning to hate you right back....

The sentiment shouldn't have come as a surprise. But it had. A surprise he didn't like much.

Not that it didn't make sense. This wasn't a popularity contest, after all. He hadn't started it to win her heart any more than he started takeovers to win friends.

But somehow he'd never factored into the equation that she'd end up hating him.

And he'd sure as hell never guessed it would bother him if she did.

But there he'd been Wednesday night, telling her he didn't want her to hate him. And meaning it.

Why should that be the case? That was the question that had been gnawing at him ever since. Why should it matter if she was beginning to hate him?

Shouldn't he count it as a sign that he was exacting his revenge? Shouldn't she hate him and resent him and feel all the things he'd felt during those years after her silence had nearly put his family on the streets?

Her getting to hate him was an indication that he was succeeding at what he'd set out to do. So, great. Terrific. Hate away!

That was what he should have been thinking. But it wasn't.

How could it be when he didn't hate her anymore?

That had been a revelation to him.

It hadn't even been something he'd realized until

the words had come out of his mouth Wednesday night.

My real problem is that I don't hate you anymore, either.

That's what he'd said. And he'd meant it, too.

But it was just as tough to accept.

He didn't hate her anymore....

If that wasn't bad enough, all he had to do to find something worse was to think about just how far from hating her he was these days.

Because not only was he physically attracted to her, not only did he enjoy her company more than he'd ever enjoyed the company of any woman, not only did he want to spend every minute concentrating on her and nothing but her, not only did he go to sleep every night with images of her in his mind's eye, but he also couldn't help admiring the way she was dealing with everything he inflicted upon her. He couldn't help being impressed by how hard she was trying to adapt to everything he threw at her. He couldn't help but appreciate the fact that she was doing every job he told her to do—no matter how loathsome or menial—without complaint. That she was working just the way she was at that moment— stoically and without so much as a trace of martyrdom.

He hadn't expected any of that from her.

The Victoria Rutherford he'd known before had been a spoiled, pampered princess who never would have endured a fraction of what she was now.

He'd been so sure he'd find her balking at every

order, whining and moaning and groaning and trying to wheedle out of any work at all.

Yet here she was, breaking her back without a peep.

And weakening his defenses at the same time because of it.

Without a peep? Was that what he'd thought?

What had Wednesday night's diatribe been if not a peep? A real big peep.

Of course he had to admit that that particular monologue hadn't been about the work. It had been about him. About him running hot and cold. About him being a jerk.

If the shoe fits, a voice in the back of his head taunted.

So, okay, maybe from her perspective he had been a pretty big jerk.

But he was entitled to some of that.

Maybe not quite as much as he'd been dishing out, but still....

But still nothing, that contrary voice countered. *You've been dishing out so much it's no wonder she's beginning to hate you.*

Beginning to hate him.

He just couldn't find a way for that to sit well.

And maybe the fact that it kept niggling at him was telling him something.

Like, you should stop being such a jerk, the voice suggested.

What did that mean? That he should stop seeking reparations? No way he was going to do that. Those reparations were his due.

But do you have to extract that due the way you have been? the voice asked. *With an iron fist and a foul disposition?*

Maybe not.

What if he did soften the tone of things somewhat? he asked himself. What would happen then?

Because every time he softened his tone, she softened hers, too. She responded to him and they ended up kissing.

Of course those were also the moments he felt the most alive. The most connected to himself, to the way he'd been once upon a time.

Those were the moments he was closer to being happy than he could remember being in a long, long while.

Those were the moments he wanted never to end.

But who knew where that might lead? Probably nowhere good.

As he slammed home nail after nail with one blow of the hammer he started to think about the alternative. About what would happen if he didn't put a moratorium on the bad attitude.

If he didn't, he concluded, before long Victoria would hate him full-bore.

And that wasn't a proposition he could live with.

So cool it and let things take their own course, that little voice in his head told him.

But would he be shortchanging his own revenge if he did?

Maybe not, if he still meted out the comeuppance sentence but just did it with more of an even temper.

After all, she'd still be there as his own private

ranch hand, learning what it was like to be on the working end of things.

But she might not grow to hate him in the process. And for some reason that suddenly seemed very important.

Besides, he admitted to himself, he was tired of fighting whatever it was that was happening between them during those good moments. Tired of fighting his own natural inclinations. Tired of fighting the present because of the past.

A past that was somehow beginning to seem farther and farther away.

But what if it meant he discovered his feelings for Victoria were something other than he'd originally thought they were? If now that he knew he didn't hate her, he discovered he felt something he didn't want to feel?

He supposed that was just a chance he'd have to take. A conflict of interest he'd just have to deal with.

Because it wasn't his feelings for her that had him worried at that moment.

It was her feelings for him.

If he could keep her from hating him full-bore by softening the tone of things and not seesawing back and forth, then it was worth it.

"Is someone coming?" Victoria said into his thoughts just then.

Adam stopped what he was doing to follow her line of vision out to the main road where so little traffic passed that the sound of an engine drew attention.

The approaching truck didn't turn onto the dirt road that led to the house. Instead it went on.

"Looks like Gavin Nighthawk on his way to the reservation," Adam said, the first civil words he'd spoken to her since their camp-out.

"He's a doctor now, isn't he? Maybe someone is sick," she responded, also for the first time without a razor's edge to her tone.

"Could be," Adam agreed.

It was strange, but that simple exchange broke the tension between them and left Adam feeling as if a ten-ton weight had just been lifted from his shoulders.

They both went back to work and he started pounding each nail in with two or three blows of the hammer rather than a single one. Victoria began to hum a sweet, soft little ditty that was a blessed improvement over the silence of the previous day and night.

Although Adam didn't know where this thing between them was headed, he did know that it was going in a different direction than he'd ever intended. For him and for her.

Something had changed in him and suddenly peace between them seemed almost as vital as vengeance.

Dr. Gavin Nighthawk was not headed for the Laughing Horse Reservation to pay a house call. He was going there for a much more troubling reason.

Or, at least, for a reason that was troubling him.

He was on his way to the isolated home of Lettie Brownbear, to visit his infant daughter.

The baby he'd fathered by Christina Montgomery.

The baby he'd delivered when he'd met Christina in the woods at her request so she could tell him only moments before she'd gone into labor that he was about to become a father.

A baby whose existence he was still having trouble coming to grips with.

One night of passion and everything had changed.

He'd been so careful up to that point, so goal-oriented. Early on he'd set his sights on finding a better life than the poverty-ridden world on the reservation where he'd grown up. Going away to college, being accepted into medical school, those had been dreams come true for him. And for his parents, who had encouraged him to reach for more.

When he'd returned to Whitehorn to do his surgical residency, he'd thought he was coming home a new man. A man with a future. A good future. Holding his own in the white world so he could obliterate his past as the Native American from the wrong side of the tracks.

It was that desire to fit into the white world that led him to make what he considered some fatal errors in judgment. Beginning with his affair with Patricia Winthrop. Pretty, popular, socially elite Patricia Winthrop—who had turned right around and spurned him.

He'd been so hurt, so angry. Such easy prey for Christina Montgomery.

Gavin had known the mayor's daughter had an eye for him. She'd made it obvious.

But he'd been in love with Patricia and had taken Christina's attentions in stride.

Until Christina had hit at just the right moment. A moment when he was so low, so lost in his own rejection by Patricia, that he'd given in to the ego-soothing balm of Christina's admiration. Her seduction.

Just one night. Just that one time.

And she'd gotten pregnant.

He hadn't had any idea.

She hadn't told him. She hadn't told anyone. And after that single night he'd kept such a distance from her that he certainly hadn't seen enough of her to guess.

But as she'd neared the end of her pregnancy she'd felt desperate enough to finally contact him.

She'd wanted his help. More help than the unexpected delivery in the woods when he'd gone to meet her.

Deep in the woods, too far from the hospital or help or even from the truck he'd had to leave out on the road, he had had no option but to deliver the baby right there.

Once he had, he'd been in a terrible bind. He hadn't been able to carry both mother and child out of the woods together.

Christina had pleaded with him to leave her there for the time being, to take the baby to safety first on the reservation, which was nearer than Whitehorn, and then come back for her.

Gavin hadn't wanted to do that but he'd had no choice. So he'd made her as warm and comfortable as he could, promised he'd return as quickly as possible and left her there.

In the woods.

Alone.

That was the last he'd seen of her, because when he'd rushed back she'd been gone.

That was the last anyone had seen of her.

Except maybe someone who might have done her harm.

That was what the sheriff was thinking now—that harm had come to Christina.

But finding her wasn't what plagued Gavin at that moment as he approached Lettie Brownbear's house. Finding Christina was out of his hands. It was the sheriff's business now. Gavin had so much more to worry about.

No, what was uppermost in his mind was that baby no one but him and Lettie knew about, and Blake Remmington, the pediatrician he'd taken her to on the sly.

That baby who had changed everything.

He'd left the baby with Lettie Brownbear, knowing she would take good care of the infant.

Lettie, an old friend of his grandmother's, wasn't the easiest person in the world to get along with and she wasn't any more fond of most people than most people were of her. So there weren't many visitors to her remote corner of the reservation.

But she'd always liked Gavin and Gavin had always liked her. Liked and trusted her. Enough so that he felt sure she would keep the secret of the baby for as long as he needed her to. For as long as it took him to figure out what was best for himself and for the child.

He'd been out to visit nearly every day in the two months since the birth and so Lettie was expecting him when he pulled up in front of her house and walked to her front door.

She called "Come in" before he'd even knocked and when he entered, he found her in the living room, sitting in a rocking chair with the baby.

Alyssa.

That's what Gavin had named the tiny baby girl, after his grandmother.

Lettie stood the moment she was sure Gavin was her visitor, nodding toward the rocking chair to let him know she expected him to take her place.

When he had, she leaned over and set the baby gently in his arms.

"She's fussy today," Lettie announced, although the infant was quiet at that moment and ordinarily had a very calm disposition. "Rock her."

Gavin did as he was told, gazing down at the cherub with her straight dark hair to match his and the chubby cheeks that were so like the baby-faced beauty of her mother.

It was obvious at one glance that Alyssa was half-white but Lettie had never commented on that fact. An odd bit of tact for the usually outspoken old woman who was known to voice her negative feelings about Anglos at the drop of a hat.

"How long are you going to leave her out here?" Lettie asked bluntly and without any preamble.

"I don't know," Gavin snapped, tired of the question she posed every time he came.

But the old, white-haired woman didn't deserve that and he curbed his temper in a hurry.

"I'm sorry," he apologized. "I just need to figure out a few things, Lettie. I need to make the right decision."

"Looks to me like you already made one wrong one."

"For myself. But now I have to think of Alyssa, too, and make the right decision for her."

"It isn't that I don't like having her," Lettie said then. "It's nice to have a baby in the house again. The checks my children send aren't the same as a warm body. But sooner or later somebody's likely to show up out here and then what? Nobody'll believe she's mine."

That was as close as Lettie ever came to making a joke, and Gavin smiled, looking her over as if her squat, matronly figure was something to behold. "Oh, I don't know. You could claim just about anything living all the way out here. Who is there to say they never saw you with any male company?" he teased.

Lettie narrowed her dark eyes at him to let him know how ridiculous she thought that was, and he conceded, returning to the subject at hand.

"I'm still just trying to get it through my head that I'm a father," Gavin confessed then, wondering how he was even functioning outside that room because he'd been so rocked by his sudden fatherhood.

"You'll find the answers," Lettie assured him, sounding very much like his late grandmother. "You're a good man, even if that face of yours does bring too many women to hang on your coattails and get you into trouble. The right way will show itself to you."

"Think so?"

"I know so. You're coming out here, taking care of that baby, aren't you? You didn't abandon it or deny it. That's why I'm doing what I'm doing, to give you the time you need. But I know you'll do right by her. Whatever it takes."

Maybe Alyssa wasn't as sure because she chose that moment to open her blue eyes, take one look at her father and start crying.

"Fussy. I told you she was fussy today," Lettie said. "I'll get a bottle."

But as the old woman left him alone with his daughter, Gavin wished he were as confident as Lettie that he'd come to the best decision over what to do about the baby.

Because at that moment he didn't have any idea how he was going to fix the mess he'd made of his life.

Adam showered first when they came in at the end of the day and by the time Victoria had finished her own shower, shampoo and had dressed again, he'd put together a pasta primavera, several slices of bruschetta and set the table for two.

He even smiled and said a friendly hello over his shoulder when she came up behind him in the kitchen.

And Victoria thought, Here we go again…

Just as they were sitting down to eat—with Adam holding her chair for her as if he were a maître d' in a five-star restaurant—the telephone rang.

"I have to get this," he said apologetically. "And if it's the conference call I should have gotten this morning, I'll have to take it. But this won't happen again."

And with that they once more ate while he was on the phone.

It was just as well, as far as Victoria was concerned. She was aware that the tension that had been swirling around them since Wednesday night had somehow diffused and she knew what that meant— all aboard the roller coaster for the next ride.

She didn't relish it. Not that she'd enjoyed the tension, either. She'd felt as if her stomach were tied into knots since their camp-out. She'd barely slept Wednesday night or Thursday, and even though she knew it was safer for her when he was showing his cold, aloof side, she couldn't help longing for the more charming Adam to reemerge.

It was just that for every time it did, she also knew there would be another time when he reversed the process, and back would come the snide, cutting, uncharming side again when she least expected it.

But one thing was certain this time, she told herself, charming or not, she wasn't going to let him get too close.

She'd meant what she'd said Wednesday night and she just would not allow herself to be sucked in by him anymore. Regardless of his mood, she was determined that she would remain on an even keel herself and keep her distance from him.

No matter what.

As the last time Adam had talked on the telephone through dinner, when he was finished eating he moved to the desk in the living room to continue his call while Victoria cleared the table.

He was still talking when she'd cleaned the kitchen and she didn't particularly want to plop down onto the couch and eavesdrop. But she also wasn't ready to go to bed, so she opted for going up to the attic for a heavy cardigan before heading out onto the porch.

It seemed as if each night was a little colder than the one before, but the brisk temperature felt good as she stepped up to the railing much as she had on her first night there.

There was something very calming about merely staring out at the lake in the distance where the nearly full moon cast its snowy reflection on the glassy surface. As she enjoyed the view, she breathed deeply of the crystal-clear air.

She hadn't been out there more than a few seconds when she realized the night wasn't exactly silent. She could hear the sorrowful mews of a cat coming from the direction of the lake.

Adam's phone call must have ended right after she'd left the cabin because he joined her then, stepping to the railing, too. He'd had on only jeans and a white polo shirt before, but now he wore that leather jacket he'd shared with her on her walk around the lake.

"I would have thought you had enough fresh air today," he said congenially.

Victoria didn't respond, instead she held up a hand that told him to be quiet and listened more intently for the mewing.

"I think there's a cat in trouble out there," she said.

Adam listened for a moment, too. "It'll be fine. Probably the barn cat."

"Maybe it's hurt."

"It sounds pitiful but not in pain."

Even pitiful was enough to make Victoria investigate. She pushed herself away from the railing and headed off the porch.

"I'm going to see if it needs help."

She expected Adam to pooh-pooh that notion, to make fun of it, to sling a sarcastic comment or two. But he just followed her as she crossed the yard in the direction of the lake.

The closer they got to it, the louder the cat's lament until they reached the shore and could see the tabby perched on a rock that protruded through the surface of the water at least ten yards out, just below the farthest stretch of the tree branches that arched overhead.

"I'll bet she crawled out on one of those limbs and fell," Victoria concluded. "And now she can't get back."

"Cats are pretty smart. She'll find her way to dry ground," Adam assured.

As if the tabby understood Adam's lack of concern, it increased the volume of its cries, sounding to Victoria as if it were pleading for assistance.

"Could we use a board or something as a ramp for her to get back?"

"No, she's too far out. I'm telling you, the way she got there, she'll get back."

"I don't think she can," Victoria insisted.

"Cats can do anything."

Victoria wanted to believe the tabby would be all right but she just didn't see how it was possible.

"Cats don't like water," she informed him.

"She liked it enough to get out there. And like it or not, if swimming is what it takes and she wants back on dry land bad enough, she'll swim."

"I don't think so," Victoria repeated.

"Well, I don't have a better suggestion. We're too far from the fire department to call them out to get a cat off a rock."

Adam hadn't said that unkindly. In fact he seemed amused by her alarm.

But that amusement dissolved when Victoria took off her sweater and handed it to him. "I'm going in after her."

"You can't do that. It's too damn cold and you're hardly dressed for a swim."

"It's just water. My clothes will dry," she said as she took off her shoes and socks.

"This is crazy—" he started to say, but by the

time the words were out of his mouth, Victoria had waded into the lake up to her knees.

Adam was right about the water being cold. Her teeth chattered, but she ignored it and continued, carefully making her way toward the cat, assuring the animal in a soothing voice that everything would be all right and hoping the lake was shallow enough to walk all the way out to the tabby and carry her back by holding her overhead.

The lake bottom was rocky and slippery so Victoria's progression was slow as she went from knee-level to hip-level to waist-level to shoulder-level. Once the water hit her chin, she didn't seem to be going any deeper as long as she stayed on the tips of her toes.

"I'm almost there," she cooed to the cat.

The mewing had stopped when she'd entered the water and the tabby had been watching Victoria's approach with interest. Victoria took that to mean that the animal knew it was about to be rescued.

But just as she was near enough to actually reach for the cat, the cat leaped almost straight up into the air, landing adeptly on the lowest tree branch, and skittered off to the ground at the base of the trunk.

Victoria closed her eyes and sighed.

From behind her she heard Adam clear his throat and she didn't have to see him to know he was trying not to laugh.

"Okay, say it. You told me so," she said as she began to turn in the water to face him once more so she could retrace her steps back to shore.

But she couldn't complete the turn.

Apparently when she'd lunged for the tabby her hair had caught on something just below the surface of the water and whatever it was was holding on tight.

"Terrific," she muttered, reaching around as best she could to free herself.

She kept at it until all the blood had drained out of both arms, and still, no matter what she did, she couldn't get loose.

"Uh, I seem to be stuck," she finally called back to Adam, wishing she could do anything but admit to him that she'd once again mishandled something.

"Your clothes?" he asked. "Just take them off."

Oh, wouldn't he like that!

Victoria was only too happy to disappoint him. "It's my hair that's caught."

Even as she answered, she tried yanking her head hard, but that didn't help, either.

"Do you mean that I'm going to have to come in there after you?" Adam asked, clearly not thrilled with the idea.

"I'm sorry. But I really am tangled up on something."

"Maybe your cat friend will come back out there and save you."

"Very funny."

"How can I be sure this isn't a trick to get even with me for being right about the cat?"

"Do you really think I'd stay out here freezing to death just for that?"

"I think it's possible, yeah."

"Well, you're wrong. If I could get out of here

I'd be back in that warm cabin getting into dry clothes.''

Silence greeted her for a moment as he seemed to weigh that reasoning.

Then he said, ''If I get out there and you aren't caught on something there'll be hell to pay.''

''Could you just hurry?''

''You're going to owe me big for this, you know.''

From the sound of his voice Victoria had the impression that he was removing his own jacket, shoes and socks as he spoke.

''Put it on my tab,'' she called back facetiously, although she realized when she did that she was the only one of them being snide. Adam was actually taking it all in stride.

She heard him come into the water and exclaim over the cold as he seemed to follow the same route she had.

''All right, let's see what kind of trouble you're in now,'' he said when he reached her.

She was shivering all over by then and her teeth were making a terrible clatter. But having him close by seemed to help some. It was almost as if his big body gave off so much heat, it even warmed the lake water.

Or maybe that was just the effect he had on her.

But one way or the other she was eager for him to release her hair so they could both get out of there.

''It looks like you're caught on a tree root,'' he said as he went to work on the task at hand. ''I'm going to have to do some pulling.''

''Okay. Just do it.''

He did, being as careful as he could and actually not hurting her as much as she'd hurt herself. But still it took him several minutes before he finally pronounced her free.

"Thanks," she said, genuinely grateful.

"Oh, sure. What's a little late night swim in our clothes in water almost cold enough to start icing over? Maybe you're hoping I'll catch my death and make you a young widow," he joked.

"That was my plan all along," she agreed as they both waded to the lake's edge where they'd started from—all under the watchful eye of the barn cat.

Once they were out of the water, they grabbed their discarded clothing and ran back to the cabin as if someone were chasing them.

"And now for the rest of this evening's entertainment..." Adam joked once they'd reached the indoors again.

Victoria was relieved to hear him make light of the incident as the heat of the cabin began to take what little effect it could under the circumstances.

They were both standing just inside the door, dripping onto the cabin's planked floor. Victoria went from assessing the puddle she was leaving to letting her gaze travel up the length of Adam—from big, squarish bare feet to long, thick legs and narrow hips hugged by wet denim that bulged in a spot she had no business looking.

When she raised her gaze she realized for the first time that he'd also taken off his shirt before coming to her rescue, so his torso was as bare as his feet.

All it took was that single sight to start wild things happening inside her.

His belly was flat and rose into that ever-broadening vee of his chiseled, muscular chest, shoulders and bulging biceps. His nipples were tiny whiskey-colored knots, and the sight of them didn't help what was happening to her in pure, primitive response to that gloriously masculine physique.

Trying to ignore her own careening senses, she yanked her eyes up to his face.

His oh-so-handsome face.

His oh-so-handsome face that wasn't exactly at an angle that allowed her to meet him eye-to-eye.

Instead he was taking in the sight of her just the way she'd been staring at him.

When she glanced down at herself she found that what he was seeing was her own pink cotton shirt shrink-wrapped to her body, leaving nothing of her lacy bra or the swell of her breasts or her taut nipples to the imagination.

"We better get dried off," she said in a voice that was unintentionally breathy.

Even though it had been unintentional, she knew the cause. Rather than being embarrassed by her exposure the way she should have been, or having the inclination to cross her arms over her chest and slouch into them for concealment, she had the inordinate urge to straighten her shoulders in invitation of something more than his heated gaze.

Adam finally dragged his eyes upward but not without what seemed like the same difficulty.

"How about I make a fire and we meet back here

to chase away the chill?'' he suggested in a voice that was as deep and quiet as hers had been breathy.

She knew it was foolhardy to agree to that when she felt what she was feeling, but she heard herself say, ''Sounds good.''

''Go on, then,'' he prodded with a poke of his chin in the direction of the stairs.

He didn't move, though.

He stayed where he was and watched her go. Watched every step she took and was still watching when Victoria reached the top of the stairs and sneaked a glance down at him.

Make an excuse and beg off, she told herself when she saw the look in his eyes even from that distance. A look of appreciation, of admiration, of hunger.

Instead she said, ''I won't be but a minute,'' before reluctantly leaving his range of vision to go into the attic bedroom.

It's just sitting by the fire, she reasoned as she peeled away her wet clothes, overlooked underwear and just pulled on plain gray sweatpants and an absolutely unsexy matching sweatshirt that zipped up the front and left a hood trailing down her back.

It's just sitting by the fire in sweats. It's not tempting fate.

But she wasn't altogether convinced of that as she toweled her hair, brushed it smooth and left it loose around her shoulders. Everything that had awakened at the sight of his naked chest left her champing at the bit to get back down to him. And no matter how much she tried to rationalize the situation, tempting fate was just what it seemed she was doing.

Still, she couldn't stop herself.

That hunger she'd thought she'd seen in Adam's eyes was echoed in her. A hunger for a little pleasant time to counteract the last two days of cold war. A hunger for sitting by that fire she could hear crackling downstairs, to sit there without the animosity that had been their companion around the fireside during their camp-out. A hunger for conversation and socializing and ending the isolation and loneliness that that cold war had made her feel.

A hunger for him.

But just for his company, she qualified firmly. Nothing more.

Talking and company were not kissing. Talking and company could be accomplished across a distance. That distance she was still sure she could maintain.

And the little dab of lip gloss she added when she'd finished brushing her hair? She only did that because her lips were parched.

Adam had changed clothes, too, by the time she got back downstairs. Like her, he'd put on a pair of sweatpants and a sweatshirt.

It was hardly striking attire, yet it did strike Victoria.

There was an intimacy in the relaxed clothing they both wore. But seeing them on Adam in particular, Victoria couldn't help feeling as if it somehow signified a tumbling of walls, a stripping away of barriers, so that what remained before her was the man alone. The essence of what he'd been all those years ago when she was so smitten by him.

With the fire raging on its own, Adam took the cushions off the couch to set in front of it. Then he turned the coffee table onto its side so they could use it as a backrest.

"I poured us some brandy," he said when he noticed her return, pointing to two small glasses of the amber liquid on the hearth. "I thought that would help get rid of the chill from the inside."

Brandy. A roaring fire. Both of them dressed in hardly anything at all. And Adam being nice and thoughtful and heart-stoppingly terrific-looking.

It was a potent combination Victoria knew she was all too susceptible to.

Still she couldn't do anything but accept the glass he offered and sit on the cushions with her back against the coffee table.

Adam sat beside her then, his long legs bent at the knees to brace his arms—the way he'd been sitting against the tree on Wednesday, watching her deal with the horses.

For some reason Victoria didn't understand, she was enthralled by the sight of his wrists—thick, strong, speckled with hair, and inexplicably sexy.

"You know," he said once they were both settled and had had several bracing sips of brandy, "I really thought I was going to get into that water and find out you were bluffing."

"It would have been a good one on you," she agreed because the note of levity in his voice—and the brandy—allowed her to relax.

"And probably just what you figure I have coming."

She merely smiled at that.

"I've had a pretty rotten disposition this week," he admitted.

"Yes, you have."

"I decided to cut it out, though. Completely."

That confession made her look at him with surprise. "You did?"

"I still intend to work you like a ranch hand. That part hasn't gone out of effect. But I think it's time the bear in me hibernates."

"How come?"

"It's wearing thin."

"You're telling me?"

He had the grace to smile. "I don't suppose you've had occasion to deal with a whole lot of contrary men, have you? You're used to them fawning over you and falling at your feet."

"Is that right?"

"I saw it for myself. All through school. Your daddy had to shoo away whole groups of them."

While I only had eyes for you, she thought but didn't say.

Instead she laughed and said, "That might have been true in school and in Whitehorn, but out in the rest of the world things aren't quite the same."

"You don't expect me to believe you can't get a date."

"Dates I can always get. But relationships that really count? That's another story."

"Are you telling me I didn't snatch you away from the love of your life?"

"Would you care if you had?"

His only answer was a negligible shrug. "I have been wondering· why you aren't married."

Why she wasn't married....

Now, there was a good question.

How could she answer it when she couldn't say it was because of her feelings for him from long ago when she was an impressionable girl? That despite what had happened, Adam had been the standard by which she'd judged all other men. A standard no one had ever been able to live up to.

How could she answer that question when she couldn't say she'd never run into another man with piercing gray eyes that seemed able to look into her soul and ignite heat with just a simple glance?

When she couldn't say she'd never found another man with a face that haunted her dreams the way his still did.

When she couldn't say she'd never encountered another man with a body quite as phenomenal. A body that seemed to draw her like a magnet. A body—if she remembered correctly from their brief coming together in that kiss in her father's barn— that seemed to have the perfect niches for her own.

How could she answer his question about why she wasn't married when she couldn't say she'd never met another man who had that certain something that he had—that same chemistry—that seemed to seep into her pores and wash away reason and rationale and most of her control?

Instead she said, "It just didn't happen. There have been a couple of guys I liked, a couple who even proposed, but it didn't go anywhere."

Before he could delve any further to discover the truth, Victoria turned the tables on him. "What about you? Why haven't you ever married?"

He thought about his answer as long as she'd considered hers before he said, "I guess I had ambition for everything but that. There hasn't ever been time. Or maybe there hasn't ever been anyone I wanted enough to spend the time on. Besides, it isn't easy— after you've had a burning obsession for someone— to go on to other women. In any serious sense, anyway."

He looked over at her then. Pointedly.

But Victoria asked anyway because she couldn't believe how that sounded. "Who were you obsessed with?"

He grinned and wrinkled his brow at the same time, as if he'd thought he was being perfectly clear. "You," he said over his brandy glass, toasting her with it.

"Me? How can that be when you barely had anything to do with me?" she asked, refuting what didn't seem possible. Hadn't she been the only one of them obsessed?

Adam finished his brandy and set the empty glass on the hearth again. Then he turned to face her, stretching one arm along the edge of the upturned coffee table behind her but without touching her.

"You were off-limits," he said. "I knew that. I was trying to play by the rules. But that didn't mean I didn't live and breathe for every glimpse of you. That I didn't know where you were and who you were with and what you were doing every minute.

That I didn't fantasize and dream about you and imagine other girls were really you when I was with them. That I didn't wake up every day hoping you'd find a way to come around, to flirt, to talk the way you did sometimes. Why else do you think I got so easily carried away in that barn that night?''

''I always thought you were just like every other guy. Some girl keeps coming around, flirting with you, preening for you, you're not going to turn your nose up at her whether you're particularly enamored or not.''

''You were more than just some girl. A whole hell of a lot more.''

It was funny but after all the years that had passed and in the situation they were now in, Victoria wouldn't have guessed that learning that Adam had actually liked her—been *obsessed* with her—could have an impact on her.

But it did.

She might as well have still been that teenage girl with the overpowering crush on the ranch hand's son at that moment—that's how much it pleased her to find out he hadn't just been going along with a good thing. Because over all the time she'd known him, all the time since she'd last seen him, she'd always thought the attraction was one-sided. That he'd only kissed her that night in the barn because she'd secretly pursued him and made herself available.

Now, to find out he'd felt the same way she had, suddenly made everything seem changed somehow. In fact, if she'd had any idea that Adam had felt for her what she'd felt for him that night, she might have had more courage to speak up in his defense. As it was, she'd thought she would be admitting that she'd chased Adam, a boy who wouldn't have given her the time of day any other way.

"You big, dumb jerk," she said endearingly.

And that was how he seemed to take it, too, because he smiled a lazy, sexy smile as his penetrating eyes held hers, searched hers, heated her from the inside out.

He leaned forward to kiss her then and in that moment when everything seemed to have changed, so did that.

Victoria didn't understand it, but she felt more free. She felt more entitled to that kiss. More deserving of indulging in that supple mouth that covered hers, that took command of hers, that urged her lips to part and her head to rest back in his cradling hand.

And indulge she did.

She answered his urging to part her lips. She met his tongue when it came to call. She let all thoughts of keeping any distance between them drift away. She let all thoughts of everything drift away so that, for the first time, she could just enjoy that moment and that kiss by that man she'd always had feelings for, feelings that seemed to burst into new life suddenly.

Without abandoning her mouth, Adam took her glass and set it somewhere else so she could reach around him when his arms wrapped her and he pulled her close.

She was only too happy to oblige. To press her

hands to the hard wall of his back, to have her breasts flattened to that broad chest that had been so magnificently bare only a short while before.

Barriers between them really had been removed because that kiss was different than any that had come before—fuller, deeper, uninhibited and alive with a hunger unleashed. That hunger she'd seen in Adam's eyes. That hunger she'd felt herself, although she'd camouflaged it and convinced herself it was something else.

But it wasn't something else. It was pure, elemental, primitive hunger to be held against his big body, to be kissed by that incredible mouth, to be carried away on the waves of all he was bringing to life inside her.

And, oh, but he was good at it!

His tongue circled and chased and danced with hers and she met the challenge. She played every game, parried every thrust and even did some chasing of her own.

Because tonight, since things had changed, she wanted so much more than they'd shared before. She *needed* so much more.

Tonight she needed to know if all her imaginings, all her fantasies about him, were true.

She found her way underneath his shirt to his back, letting her palms glaze the tight satin of flesh over hard muscle, digging her fingers into the glory of that powerful expanse. Massaging his shoulders, his biceps, his sides, even daring to dip only her fingertips into the waistband of his sweatpants.

Maybe it was the insistence of that massage or the

almost-frenzy that accompanied it, but Adam seemed to get the message that she needed more than kissing, no matter how wonderful the kissing was.

He slid the zipper of her sweatshirt down, just enough to slide one hand in to the side of her neck, caressing it with leisurely strokes that slowly eased downward, leaving a trail of delight until he finally reached her breast, closing that big hand around the burgeoning globe that had been crying out for just that.

Their kisses grew urgent and openmouthed as that adept hand did the most incredible, magical things to her. He found the tight kernel of her nipple with gentle fingers that traced around and around it, tugging, teasing, tormenting and then smoothing with a hot, tender palm until he drove her so wild she couldn't help letting her head fall away from his kiss so she could gasp for the air she needed to moan in pleasure.

. But Adam went on kissing her. The soft, sensitive underside of her chin, the arched column of her neck, the hollow of her throat, and lower still. He kissed a long, slow path to the swell of her breast, where the kisses stopped and only the tip of his tongue trailed the rest of the way until that glorious mouth captured her nipple, engulfing it in warm, moist velvet splendor. Sucking. Tugging with tender teeth. Flicking his talented tongue against the pebbled crest.

He eased her to lie back on the cushions, going with her so that the length of his body followed every curve of hers.

Victoria could feel the proof of just how much he wanted her making its presence known at her hip.

His hands seemed to be everywhere then—on her breasts, on her side, on her stomach where he slipped below the border of her sweatpants just far enough to reach a finger into her navel.

This is it, she silently rejoiced. He's going to make love to me…

And she was willing. She wanted him to make love to her. She wanted to finally know what she'd only been dreaming about for what seemed like forever.

But that was when he stopped.

Not easily—that was clear. But more as if some greater force had yanked him away by the scruff of his neck.

Because all of a sudden he was gone.

He was up on one elbow, pulling up the zipper of her sweatshirt in a fast swipe before he dropped his head to hers and sighed a sigh that blew a hot gust of air into her ear.

"Time. We should take our time," he said in a passion-raspy voice.

Victoria couldn't help but hope he only meant to slow things down, maybe to move them into the bedroom, not to end them.

But those hopes were dashed when he pushed himself into a sitting position, then took her hands to pull her up, too, and said, "I think you ought to go to your room now. While I can still let you."

Victoria raised her chin at him, tempted to refuse to go. Tempted to stay to see if he'd start again what every ounce of her being was crying out for him to finish.

But a tiny speck of common sense told her not to do that. It told her to cool off. To give herself that time he'd mentioned to think about what she'd learned tonight. To digest it before she took that final step from which there would be no return for either of them.

So she didn't stay.

She stood, said a simple good-night that was almost inaudible, and headed for the stairs.

She only got as far as the second step when the sound of his voice stopped her.

"What do you say tomorrow we get away from here for a while? Go into Whitehorn? Have dinner?"

"Okay," she agreed, only partially aware of what he'd said, while a bigger part of her waited for him to invite her back in front of that fire.

But he didn't. When he didn't say anything more, she finally climbed the stairs to the attic.

Even in her solitary bed moments later she could still feel Adam's hands on her skin. His mouth on hers. The long, hard staff of his desire for her pressed so unmistakably to her side....

And she knew that in spite of the fact that he'd left her frustrated and unfulfilled and craving a completion of what he'd begun, this hadn't been any kind of cruel game on his part.

He'd wanted her every bit as much as she'd wanted him.

She just didn't know why he hadn't followed through with it

Seven

There couldn't have been a more beautiful late-October day for a trip into Whitehorn. When Victoria and Adam set off after lunch the next afternoon, the sun was high in a perfectly clear blue sky.

Victoria also couldn't have asked for better company than Adam, who was showing her yet another side of himself today. A side that was pure, winning charisma.

Neither of them had brought up what had happened the night before since encountering each other again this morning. In fact they both acted as if nothing at all had happened.

It left Victoria still confused about why Adam had put a premature end to what she'd thought was headed for lovemaking. But she'd decided there was no sense rocking the boat by pursuing explanations.

Some things were better just left alone.

As Adam drove, he played tour guide, bringing Victoria up to date on which pieces of property had changed hands and why, pointing out what had been improved upon, reminding her of long-ago mischief enacted here and there when they and their friends were teenagers and had time on their hands.

It was fun for Victoria and it made the trip into town go fast.

The Stop-n-Swap was where they went first once they reached Whitehorn. Adam had decided Victoria needed a warmer coat.

It struck her as strange that he still opted for the Stop-n-Swap as the place to buy that coat—in keeping with his original aim of humiliating her—when he was being so charming and considerate and entertaining that he was making their outing seem like a really great Saturday afternoon date.

But she was having too good a time to point out the discrepancy and besides, she was looking forward to seeing Crystal Cobbs again.

There were only two other people at the Stop-n-Swap when Victoria and Adam arrived—Crystal, who was arranging pairs of shoes on a table, and Sloan Ravencrest, who was browsing not far away.

Although what the deputy was browsing for seemed questionable to Victoria because despite the fact that his hands were moving hangers of shirts around a rack, his dark eyes were only on Crystal.

And in those dark eyes was an unmistakable interest.

An interest that Victoria thought might be returned when she saw Crystal cast a glance of her own over her shoulder at Sloan while she seemed oblivious to Victoria and Adam.

It was actually Sloan who noticed them before Crystal did, snapping to attention as if he'd been caught at something he wasn't supposed to be doing.

"Hey. Hi," he said to them somewhat anxiously.

They both returned his hello and then Adam bent to speak into Victoria's ear, "Why don't you look around and I'll let Sloan know we didn't come across any sign of Christina Montgomery when we were out rounding up the horses."

"Okay," Victoria agreed, trying not to like the feel of having him that close to her, the feel of his warm breath against her skin, as much as she did.

As Adam went off to talk to the deputy, Crystal finally seemed to become aware that she had customers and headed for Victoria with a welcoming smile.

Crystal really was pretty, Victoria thought, with her raven-black hair and porcelain skin and sparkling green eyes. It was no wonder Sloan was attracted to her.

But then it was also no wonder Crystal was attracted to the deputy, whose longish dark hair, dark eyes and lean, well-muscled body could turn any woman's head.

Well, maybe any woman except Victoria, who still thought Adam was more handsome as she looked at the two men clasping hands.

"Is the honeymoon over?" Crystal asked by way of greeting when she reached Victoria.

Victoria didn't want to tell her it hadn't ever begun so she just said, "Mmm," and hoped the other woman would take that as an answer. Then she told Crystal what she'd come looking for and Crystal showed her what coats were available.

But as Victoria tried on a few, she couldn't resist nodding in the direction of the men. "I think our deputy is a little sweet on you. Is something going on between you guys?''

''Between Sloan Ravencrest and me?'' Crystal asked as if the very idea shocked her. ''No. Of course not.''

Crystal had said that pretty convincingly. But she gave herself away when, a moment later, she said, ''Why would you think he's sweet on me?''

''He couldn't take his eyes off you until he realized he had an audience in Adam and me. It certainly didn't seem as if it was a shirt he was really looking for over there.''

''Oh, I'm sure it was.''

''And he keeps sneaking glimpses of you even now,'' Victoria informed her with another subtle glance at the men.

''Maybe he just needs help with something. Or maybe I have something stuck in my teeth…''

Victoria laughed. ''You don't.''

The choice of coats was slim so Victoria settled on a heavy wool pea coat, seeing that more of Crystal's attention was still on Sloan than on the sale she was about to make.

''Looks like maybe you're a little sweet on the deputy, too,'' Victoria said when she'd asked Crystal the price of the coat three times without an answer.

''No…I don't…I mean, I'm not… We hardly know each other,'' Crystal finally responded.

''Maybe it's time you *got* to know each other.''

''Oh, I don't think so…''

Adam's chat with Sloan seemed to end just then

and he came over to Victoria and Crystal, putting an end to their conversation.

After the coat had been paid for and Adam was headed away from the cash register, Victoria leaned over it and whispered to Crystal, "At least go over and ask if you can help him."

"No, no, I—" Crystal's cheeks pinkened just enough to let Victoria know her hunch about the two of them was right. "That's not necessary."

"Are you matchmaking?" Adam asked in an aside as they left.

It did seem kind of silly, when she thought about it, because she'd been acting like some old married lady fostering young love. Some old married lady who was so happy in her own life that she wanted others to be just as happy.

But for some reason that was sort of how she felt.

"I was just pointing out that the deputy seemed to have an eye for Crystal."

"That's matchmaking," Adam concluded, but the sly smile he cast her gave a stamp of approval that almost made it seem as if he was all for other people feeling the way he did at that moment, too.

And Victoria couldn't help thinking, Oh what a difference a week can make....

After leaving the Stop-n-Swap, Adam took Victoria to the high school football field where the local team was playing and a fair portion of Whitehorn's citizens were gathered to watch, whether they knew anyone in particular on the team or not. Supporting youth sporting events was a big pastime of townsfolk and it brought back fond memories for Victoria of her own days as a cheerleader.

Together she and Adam were drawn into the excitement just like everyone else, cheering on the home team with as much enthusiasm as the parents in the stands all around them.

When it was over—with Whitehorn the winner—Victoria and Adam did some grocery shopping and then Adam took her to the Hip Hop for dinner.

Only, unlike the meal they'd eaten at the café the previous Sunday before leaving town, this time they talked and laughed and were so interested in each other that they barely noticed anyone else in the restaurant.

Dusk was falling when they headed back to the ranch and as Victoria sat on the passenger end of the truck's bench seat, she had to fight the oddest inclination to slide across so she could be closer to Adam.

Okay, so they'd had a great day and they'd flirted and teased and talked as if they really had been out on a date. But that didn't mean what naturally followed was for her to snuggle up next to him on the way home.

Even if Adam had taken her hand to climb down from the bleachers at the football game and had laid his palm along the small of her back as he'd ushered her in or out of doors.

Even if she couldn't keep her eyes off his chiseled profile, or the way he filled out the dove gray Western shirt he wore, or the way his massive, jeans-clad thighs were spread against the seat, or how his hands mastered the steering wheel without effort—much like they'd mastered her flesh, her breasts, the night before.

No, there was not a reason for her to snuggle up against his side for the drive home like some lovesick teenager, she reiterated to herself.

In fact, those were all reasons for her not to. They were reasons for some decorum to be reestablished.

Which meant that she stayed hugging the passenger door and just thinking about how good it would feel to have those few feet that separated them closed.

"So," Adam said into her thoughts as they hit the open road, "I'm betting that marrying me wasn't in the game plan for your future. But what was?"

It took Victoria a moment to concentrate on the words rather than just letting the whiskey of his voice intoxicate her in the dim interior of the vehicle; a moment to remind herself that the intimacy they were sharing now that they were alone had to be kept in perspective.

"What did I have planned for my future?" she repeated as she organized her thoughts.

"That was the question, yeah."

"Let's see, I'm halfway to earning my Ph.D. I had plans to finish that and hopefully get a full professorship under my belt. I also thought I'd get married, have kids, a dog, a house with a white picket fence—the usual stuff."

"But you said last night that there wasn't anybody you were serious about," he reminded.

"That doesn't mean I didn't think someone would come along eventually."

He nodded solemnly and she couldn't be sure why he appeared to dislike that answer.

"What about you?" she asked. "What were your plans for the future? Or was retribution all you had on your agenda?"

She'd said that half jokingly, but he still frowned over at her, as if he didn't want that brought into the discussion. Then he said, "I guess I thought I'd probably get married someday, too. Have kids. In an abstract way, you know? It wasn't on my to-do list, just something I assumed would happen down the road. I mean, I didn't imagine myself a lonely old codger without a family at the end of my life. But mainly my focus was all on work."

"All work and no play…"

He took his eyes off the road to glance at her again, this time with a one-sided smile. "Are you telling me I'm dull?"

She just shrugged as if to say maybe.

He laughed at the silent jab.

"How exciting would Mr. Right have to be?"

"Oh, pretty exciting," she said with exaggeration that bordered on bluster.

"In what way?"

"He'd have to be intelligent and funny and ambitious and energetic and witty and sensitive and kind and generous and—"

"Able to leap tall buildings in a single bound—"

"And he'd have to love to dance," Victoria added as the cherry on top.

"No wonder you were still single," he teased wryly, as if her list were impossible to satisfy.

"Good thing I swooped in and forced some reality on you."

Victoria rolled her eyes at him. "This is reality?" she joked back.

He held out one arm. "Want to pinch me and see?"

She wanted to do a whole lot more than pinch him. She wanted to caress those bulging biceps and slip underneath his shirt to lie her cheek against his chest....

But she put her efforts into yanking her wandering thoughts back into line instead.

"How about Ms. Right?" she asked. "What did you have in mind?"

"All of the above. And then some." He let that last part come out full of innuendo as he turned his pewter-gray eyes on her again to give her a lascivious once-over.

And then a question that had been taunting Victoria for the last week popped out of her mouth before she even knew she was going to ask it. "What about now, are your thoughts about marriage still only in the abstract?"

"You mean now that you and I are actually married do I have a more solid image of my future? Of a future for *this* marriage?"

"Yes, I guess that is what I mean," she confirmed, wishing she hadn't said the words because the subject was too sobering to have a place in what had only been inconsequential small talk up to then.

But the question couldn't be recalled now that it

was out there and so there was nothing she could do but wait for him to say something.

He wasn't in any hurry to reply. They'd probably driven a quarter of a mile before he finally said, "I don't know what the future holds for you and me and the marriage. Making you marry me is about as rash an act as I've done in my life. Well, maybe with the exception of kissing you in your father's barn that night you got me into trouble. When I instigated this thing, I figured it would go on for however long it took to get the anger and resentment out of my blood. But now…"

His voice dwindled off and the silence that was left said he didn't know how to finish that thought.

There wasn't anything Victoria could think to say, either, so she left him to what looked like his own musings on the matter.

But it didn't take him long to work through whatever those musings were before he said, "I suppose it isn't outside the realm of possibility for us to evolve into the real thing and end up growing old together. Is it?"

"I don't know," she answered honestly. In truth, while she wondered frequently how much longer this marriage might go on, she'd never thought about what she actually wanted to happen.

Adam didn't let the more somber state they'd fallen into stay for long before he cast her a devilish glance that lightened things up again. "Mr. Right has to dance, huh?"

Victoria didn't know what Adam had up his sleeve—besides muscles enough to drive her crazy—

but the glint of mischief in his eyes told her he was up to something.

She didn't mind. She was all too willing to shy away from the more serious thoughts of the future, too, and get back to just having a good time the way they had been before she asked that fatal question there didn't seem to be an answer to. So she played along.

"Mr. Right? He definitely has to dance," she confirmed.

"Square dance? Line dance? Ballroom?"

"Nothing fancy."

Adam nodded and pulled the truck over to the side of the road, turning off the engine.

Then he pointed an index finger at her and looked down the length of it straight into her eyes. "'Nothing fancy' I can do."

He flipped on the truck's radio, fiddled with the dial until he found some slow country-western music, then hopped out of the cab and came around to her side to open her door.

"But I can do it under the stars," he said as if he were upping the ante. He took her hand and pulled her out with him.

Neither of them had on a coat and since dark had fallen and they were nearer to the mountains than Whitehorn, it was chilly.

But Victoria barely noticed as Adam swung her into his arms there on the soft shoulder of the road.

Spending the day in town had been a treat, so she was wearing a navy-blue knit dress for the occasion. It was no protection from the cold but it allowed her to feel the heat of his body radiating through it. And that heat and having him close enough to share it felt so terrific she wouldn't have changed a thing.

The stars he'd promised were just beginning to come out in a still cloudless sky. There were no streetlights to mar the white glow of the moon. Crickets seemed to chirp in harmony with the music from the radio. The slightest breeze hummed through the open fields on either side of the country road. And Victoria finally got her wish to press her cheek against the rock-solid wall of Adam's chest.

How could the future matter when the present was so good? she asked herself, closing her eyes so she could just drift along on Adam's smooth lead.

There was definitely nothing fancy about his dancing, but that didn't matter, either. She'd only been teasing about it being a requirement for Mr. Right because most men she knew balked at the very suggestion.

It was bliss to be in Adam's arms. To feel his strong hand on her back. To have his other hand holding hers in a cotton-soft embrace between his shoulder and hers. To have his head resting against her loose-falling hair and be bathed in the warmth of his breath. To have the scent of his after-shave wafting around her. To be warmed solely by the heat of his body. To hear his heartbeat while her own pulse kept the same rhythm.

As she sank into the pure pleasure of it all, something strange happened.

She relaxed more completely than she ever had in her life. Every care, every tension, every worry, seemed to drain away. Every doubt, every question, every fear, evaporated. Nothing had ever felt as right as being there in that niche of his body that seemed carved just for her.

He raised his head from hers then and said in a quiet, husky voice, "Do I pass, Teach?"

Victoria smiled and lifted her face from his chest to look up at him. "B-plus," she decreed as her eyes feasted on his striking face etched in moonlight.

He smiled down at her, a slow, sensual smile. "Good enough," he said as if accepting an offer.

Then the smile eased into a more solemn expression and he bent to kiss her even as they still swayed to the music on the radio.

She knew his kiss by then, but familiarity took nothing away from it. There was no doubt about it—the man could kiss!

His mouth took charge of hers, guiding, teasing, exploring, cherishing.

His lips were parted and this time it required no urging for hers to do the same. When his tongue came to play, to entice, to seduce, hers was only too willing to oblige.

He let go of her hand so he could wrap both arms around her and Victoria did likewise, happy to have her own arms full of his big, masculine body, her hands riding the mountainous muscles of his back.

Her nipples hardened against his chest in response to what that kiss ignited inside her. In response to him and to what this might be the beginning of. In anticipation of feeling his touch again.

Maybe we'll go back to the truck, she thought. Maybe he'll make love to me right here....

At that moment she didn't care about the logistics. She didn't care if they were out in the open on the side of the road.

She only cared about what he was bringing to life within her with that deep, deep kiss and hands that caressed her shoulders, her back, the base of her spine.

Hands that grasped her rear end and pulled her up against more of that proof that he wanted her....

And then, as he'd done the previous evening, he stopped.

Again.

Again he seemed reluctant. He seemed to struggle mightily for control, for the strength and willpower to end what was on the verge of being something as wonderful as it had been the night before.

But he still stopped.

"I think I should take my B-plus and get us home," he said, joking in a voice that was raw and ragged and sounded the way Victoria felt.

Then he just let go of her, without giving her a chance to say anything that might keep him there.

He did take hold of her hand, though, to lead her back to the truck where he opened the passenger door and helped her up once more.

Victoria didn't know what she would have said even if he'd given her the opportunity. She was too frustrated, too churned up inside to know what to say, except maybe to beg him not to do this, not to get her all worked up and then leave her aching for a completion that never came.

She couldn't do that. She wouldn't beg him or even let him know just how much of an ache he'd left her with at least twice now.

So instead, once more feeling stunned and stung and confused, she just sat hugging the passenger's side door the way she had been before, watching Adam round the front of the truck—jamming his hands through his hair hard enough to hurt and looking as if he needed the pain for some reason.

He climbed back in behind the wheel and started the engine, causing a brief blip in the radio that then went right on playing the slow, sexy country music they'd been dancing to.

Only now it grated on Victoria and she reached out and turned it off.

Adam cast a glance in the direction of the radio, but not at her. He didn't say anything. He just drove the rest of the way to the ranch in silence.

Silence that seemed to Victoria to be charged with things that needed to be said.

Certainly it was charged with things she wanted to say.

But as they unloaded the truck of the day's purchases, there was a part of her that told her to just let it go, to not let him know what he was doing to her.

Unfortunately there was another part of her that couldn't do that and she finally exploded, throwing a bag of cotton balls at him as he turned from stocking the cabinets.

"I said it at the camp-out and I meant it. Keep your hands—and your kisses—to yourself."

Okay, so the command was not only belated at that point, but it also rang a little false when she'd participated willingly both of the times he'd come near her since the camp-out.

But she was so filled with pent-up anger and unsatisfied arousals that she wasn't thinking clearly.

Adam had caught the cotton balls before they'd hit him and now set them calmly on the counter before he leaned his hips against its edge and looked at her with a funereal expression.

"This isn't a game or part of the comeuppance the way you're thinking it is," he said in a voice to match his countenance.

"You're just toying with me," she accused. "Getting even."

"No, I'm not. I wanted—" He jammed another punishing hand through his hair, the way he'd done out on the road. "Believe me, I'm not toying with you or getting even when it comes to…not keeping my hands to myself."

"Then what are you doing?" she shouted.

"Suffering like hell at the moment," he said under his breath with his head turned away from her, closing his eyes as if he really were being tortured.

He took a deep breath, held it, then blew it out and looked at her again.

"I couldn't let things go where they were going, tonight or last night," he said.

"Why not?" she demanded, not aware of how it sounded until she said it. But everything inside her was in such a jumble, such turmoil, she was just one raw exposed nerve.

"Making love to you would have been turning a corner I didn't know if I should turn," he said after a while of what appeared to be a debate over whether or not to let her in on what he was thinking. "I made you marry me to get back at you and your family. To teach you a lesson in what it's like to be powerless. To be at someone else's mercy. But making love? That's different. That has to be different. It can't be a power thing. It can't be something that happens because you're at someone else's mercy. I don't want you that way."

The man had as much of a knack for shocking her as he had for kissing her. Because of all the things she'd thought might be behind his abrupt endings the last two nights, that hadn't been one of them.

"Did you feel like you were forcing me?"

"No. But I didn't know what was going through your head, either. I didn't know if you felt like you had some kind of duty or obligation."

Duty and obligation. Being powerless and at his mercy. No, none of those should have any part in making love.

But they certainly hadn't been what she'd been feeling when she was in his arms.

Yet now, when the tidal wave of passion wasn't carrying her away, it occurred to her that if she let him know she hadn't been feeling any of that, that she'd just plain wanted him, she was taking a bigger step than she'd realized. A step she shouldn't take lightly.

After all, this was a man who had coerced her into marriage as a payback. A man who hadn't exactly been a peach to her during the last week.

It crossed her mind that maybe she shouldn't let him know how she felt about him or that he could arouse so much in her that she forgot everything else.

But there he was, only a few feet away from her, with that black hair and those incredible features and those pewter eyes and that body to die for.

There he was, the man who had grown from the boy who had first captured her young girl's heart from a distance.

Somehow that was all she saw now. Not the arrogant, ruthless corporate raider who had set out to make her just another of his cold, calculated takeovers.

What she saw was a man with an unexpectedly vulnerable side. A man who, despite his own old hurts and grudges, still had a side that was sensitive and caring and conscientious enough to not make love to her under the slightest hint that it might not be what she wholeheartedly wanted.

But it was what she wanted. Wholeheartedly.

He was what she wanted.

The only way she would have him, though, was if she let him know it.

"I have felt powerless and at your mercy," she said then, no longer shouting, all the anger gone from her voice. "And I've felt a duty and an obligation, too. But last night and tonight, when you kissed me, none of those things were what I was feeling or even thinking about. They weren't there at all. Not for me.''

And that said, she turned and left him to think about it.

She went to the stairs and climbed them to the attic, going into her room and wondering the whole way if Adam would follow.

Wanting him to follow....

And then she heard his footsteps on the stairs. Her heart started to pound and she could hardly breathe even as a little voice in her head said, *What if he's just coming to say he still doesn't think you should turn that corner?*

She'd left her bedroom door open to the narrow hallway between it and the staircase, so she saw Adam the moment he reached the top.

He was frowning, and fear welled up in Victoria. Fear that he might reject her, that payback really might be what was going on. Fear that he might not want her as much as she wanted him.

He came all the way into the room, stopping only when he was standing directly in front of her with a scant hair breadth between them.

But he didn't touch her.

''If I'd met you again and we'd spent some pleasant time together, getting to know each other, catching up, and none of what's gone on this week had happened, and you were free as a bird, would we be standing in your bedroom right now?''

So he needed to be absolutely sure.

As sure as she was.

Victoria felt relief wash through her and she

smiled up at him. "Yes," she said quietly, forcefully, because she meant it. Because if they'd met again and rediscovered that old flame and ended up in her bedroom the way they were now, it would have been a fantasy come true.

He held her eyes with his, searching them as if for confirmation.

Maybe he found it because he reached out, running his hands from her wrists along the sleeves of her dress. Then he clasped her shoulders and pulled her to him, capturing her mouth in a wide-open kiss that picked up where they'd left off on the roadside.

That was all it took to make her blood run through her veins like a raging river, to tighten her nipples all over again, to make her put her arms around him.

He held her close, cradling her head in one hand because the kiss was so intense her neck was craned backward beneath it.

If there had been hunger in any kiss before, it was nothing like this one. Now their hunger, and every bit of the desire, the yearning, that had simmered below the surface in them both, was unleashed. Now every inhibition vanished and a primitive abandon took over.

Neither of them seemed to be able to get enough of the other. Adam's tongue didn't tease. It came to greet hers in pure, sensual aggression, letting her know he meant business. He held her in such a vise-like grip, it was as if he thought he might lose her. And again, when his hips met hers, there was a sharp, insistent ridge that told her just how much he wanted her.

No more, no less, than she wanted him as all the unmet needs she'd tamped down sprang to life, as all the age-old pining awakened as if from a long sleep.

She was holding on to him just as fiercely as he was holding her. Kissing him just as avidly. Just as deeply. Just as aggressively.

When he unzipped the back of her dress, she let him know that being rid of clothing was a fine idea by kicking off her shoes and yanking his shirttails out of his waistband, then pulling at the snaps of his shirtfront until each of them opened.

From there, clothes fell away beneath the onslaught of fingers and hands that made fast work of shedding them even as mouths still clung together and kissed and played and almost warred in the fervor that was passion too long held in check and now liberated. Passion that was urgent and powerful and demanding. Passion that swept everything out of its path until they were both naked. Until bodies could come together, bare flesh to bare flesh.

Then his mouth abandoned hers and he scooped her up into his arms, carrying her to the double bed that had seemed so lonely all week, lying her on the downy comforter that covered it.

For only a split second before he joined her, she got to look at him. At the glory of his naked body in all its masculine magnificence.

And it was magnificent! So magnificent it took her breath away as her eyes traveled from broad, straight shoulders down impeccable pectorals to his flat stomach and lower still to narrow hips, to the essence of his manhood.

But the visual feast lasted only a second before he was there on the bed beside her, with a heavy thigh across hers and his lips rekindling that kiss as if he'd been starved for it.

Only now while one arm braced him to stay above her, his other hand was free.

Free to smooth the side of her face.

Free to sweep along her jaw.

Free to caress her neck, her throat, the sensitive hollow of her collarbone.

Free to reach her breast, engorged and straining for his touch.

His dexterous, skillful, ardent touch.

His hand was big and warm and only slightly calloused. Tender and teasing. Molding and massaging, until her nipple was a stone he rolled beneath his palm.

Her spine arched all on its own in answer to the symphony of sensations he was erupting within her, escaping his kiss even though that hadn't been her intent.

But he didn't desert her. Instead he rained kisses down the same path his hand had taken moments before, stopping when he reached her breast again, to kiss oh-so-softly just the striving peak.

Such tender torment when she wanted so much more. Needed so much more.

And then he gave it, taking her breast into his mouth, flicking, circling her nipple with the hot velvet of his tongue.

But still it wasn't enough. It wasn't enough of him.

She let her hands begin their own quest. They glided down his back, all sinew and tendons and strength. Glazed his derriere, taut and tensed. Slid from his hips to his thighs, massive and muscular.

Then she let her hand trail upward just enough to take hold of that long, hard staff that left no doubt what was going on inside him, closing around his thick, unyielding potency, learning the heat and power there, learning just how wild she could drive him.

But he could give as good as he got because the palm that rested on her stomach suddenly began a slow descent of its own.

A descent that raised goose bumps of longing across her skin. That sparked glittering anticipation that opened her legs in invitation.

He reached her. He cupped her. He caressed her with silken strokes and seeking fingers that found their way inside, that found that one special spot that took her need, her craving, her desire, to a point past sanity or rational thought. A point past bearing.

And then he was above her, that incredible body was between her thighs as his mighty shaft searched for a home and found it inside her. He filled her with hard, hot flint-like strength and made her feel as if, only in that instant, she'd been made whole.

She moved with him at first, keeping pace, tightening muscles around him, taking him completely into her and releasing her hold only reluctantly, only because she knew he would come back again.

But as he went faster and faster, she couldn't keep

up. She could only cling to him, to the vast expanse of his back, and ride along as those earlier sparks of anticipation took flame, burning brighter and brighter, blazing to life with an intensity she'd never known before, until it was as if a thunder flash struck and she surged into the radiant white hot light of ecstasy. The feeling was so pure and clean and so powerful she couldn't breathe, she couldn't do anything but let it explode inside her.

It exploded inside her just the way Adam had, as every muscle in his body seemed to tense to its limit and he went rigid above her, plunging so deeply into her they were melded together in that one, perfect moment of unfathomable bliss.

And then it began to ebb, to slip down the other side of the slope.

Victoria could feel Adam relaxing muscle by muscle. She could feel her own pulse slowing beat by beat. She could hear each of them breathing again as if they'd both stopped when time had seemed suspended and they'd drawn their life force from the other's body rather than from air.

Adam laid his forehead to hers and kissed her nose.

Then he slipped his arms under her so that when he rolled to his side she went with him.

He held her, close and tight, their bodies still one, their hearts beating in unison.

Their marriage had been sealed.

Although neither of them said anything, Victoria hoped that they really had turned a corner.

Because somewhere in the process of making love,

something had flooded out of the deepest recesses of her. Something warm and wonderful and long held secret.

Something that gave her over to Adam body and soul.

And left her really, truly, within his power and at his mercy now.

Eight

Victoria woke up early the next morning when bright sunshine flooded through the dormer window straight into her eyes. She hadn't closed the curtains.

But then, she'd had other things to occupy her thoughts. And every other part of her, too.

She was lying on her side, facing the window, and the cause of her forgetfulness was lying right behind her.

Adam.

His knees were in the lee of her knees; his thighs were a seat for her thighs; his torso was her backrest; his right arm was around her, running the length of her right arm; his left arm stretched above them both; and his chin rode the top of her head on the pillow they shared.

Spoons.

It was nice. Incredibly nice.

So nice that Victoria thought she could sleep every night and wake up every morning like that for the rest of her life.

And she wondered if she'd have the chance.

She wondered how making love—three times before they'd slept—would change things between them.

She wondered if making love was enough to alter the whole course of their lives. Enough to wipe away the harm done in the past.

She couldn't help hoping that it was. Hoping that things might actually work out for them.

She cared for Adam in a way that wouldn't be denied any longer. She cared for him in a way that scared her too much to put a name to it. That scared her because now that making love had opened the door to it, she was all the more susceptible to him, all the more unprotected from him.

He could hurt her now and she knew it. He could devastate her. He could devastate her as badly as she had devastated him and his family all those years ago.

While the biggest part of her didn't believe he would, didn't believe that anything as wonderful, as soul-uniting as what they'd done the night before could have come from a need for retribution or could have left them anything but close, there was still a small part of her that worried what the daylight might bring. That tortured her with tiny flashes of images of him smirking at her all over again and telling her this whole thing—this whole seduction—had all been one grand act to get her to completely and totally let down her guard and open herself to him body, mind and spirit so that, just when she had, he could pull the rug out from under her and truly hurt her.

She didn't want to think about that. She wouldn't think about it, she decided. She wouldn't let it damage the pleasure of waking up in Adam's arms, of feeling his big body curved around her, of having the warmth of his breath in her hair.

She closed her eyes and just reveled in that moment, in all the sensations, in the cocoon he formed around her.

Everything would be all right, she told herself. Better than all right. Everything from here on would be great.

Hadn't he said himself that he'd thought about this marriage evolving into the real thing? About growing old together?

Stranger things had happened than two people coming together under less than ideal circumstances and still making it work.

They were married, after all. Their lives had been joined even before their bodies, long ago, when they were teenagers, and it took until now for them to find their way to each other.

Now that they had, maybe this could be the beginning for them. The real beginning. Maybe now they could get to know the people they'd grown up to be. They could make plans. They might even have kids eventually. Kids who would have kids and they could tell them about the inauspicious wedding that had formed the roots for a whole family.

Everything would be all right, she repeated in her mind as if it were a magic spell. Everything would be better than all right. Everything from here on would be great.

She took a deep breath and sighed it out, picturing the home they would build, the babies they would have together, the nights they would spend like the last one.

She opened her eyes, thinking that maybe she'd wake Adam and greet the morning the way they'd passed the night.

But for no particular reason, when her eyes were open again, her glance happened onto something she hadn't noticed before.

The dormer window rose from the attic floor so she had a certain amount of view of the roof. And in that view she spotted the hammer she'd used when she and Adam had repaired the shingles on Friday. Apparently she'd forgotten it.

It was no big deal, but that niggling negative part of her taunted her with the possibility—however remote—that if Adam realized her oversight he might turn once again into that sarcastic, condescending, snide bear he'd been so much of this past week.

Sure he'd said he'd put that bear into hibernation and she hadn't seen any signs of it since. But she just didn't want to take any chances. She didn't want anything to mar what was between them now.

Suddenly, retrieving that hammer and putting it away before Adam knew it was out there seemed like a good idea.

Then, once she had, she could crawl back into this warm bed and wake Adam up.

She was near the edge of the mattress so she just rolled forward, carefully easing herself out from under Adam's arm.

He was sleeping soundly—she could hear it in his deep breathing—and although his arm ended up without a prop and his hand dangled off the side of the bed, he didn't stir.

His shirt was on the floor not far away and Victoria snatched it up, slipping into it and closing the snaps down the front. Quietly she pulled on sweatpants and tennis shoes, careful not to wake him.

She wanted that pleasure all to herself after she'd put the hammer away.

She wanted it even more when the scent of his after-shave wafted up from the fabric of his shirt and the feel of it against her naked skin reminded her of having his big body all around her.

She tiptoed to the window, thinking briefly about going out onto the roof that way. But not only would opening it make a certain amount of noise, she could tell just how cold it was outside from the frost on the corners of the glass and the thin sheet of white that covered the roof, and she didn't want a blast of frigid air waking him if the noise didn't.

Instead she tiptoed quietly out of the attic bedroom, down the stairs and out the cabin's back door.

Adam had brought the ladder from the barn on Friday but Victoria had seen where he'd put it when they were finished so she went directly there to get it.

It wasn't hard to manage as she toted it around to the front of the cabin and propped it against the edge of the porch overhang.

All she was thinking the whole time was that it was only a matter of minutes before she'd accomplished her goal and Adam would never be the wiser about her forgetfulness.

Then she'd retrace her steps—well, maybe she'd stop in the bathroom to brush her teeth first—and before he even knew she'd been gone she'd slip back under the covers with him. She'd snuggle her naked body to the warm splendor of his. She'd wake him with slow, sexy kisses. She'd let her hands do the things she now knew would turn him on.

With the ladder in place, Victoria climbed it in a hurry. A big hurry since just thinking about her plans to turn on Adam had turned her on, too.

She moved in such a hurry that she didn't stop to consider that the frost on the roof might make it slippery. Too slippery to be up there.

No sooner had her feet hit the shingles than they went out from under her.

She lost her balance, sliding uncontrollably toward the edge, struggling for anything to grab on to. But there wasn't anything except the ladder. When she caught hold of it, she only increased her downward momentum, pushing it away from the roof as she went completely over the edge and plummeted to the earth below.

Adam wasn't sure what woke him.

A thud was what it seemed like. From outside.

He didn't give it much thought. He just rolled over and reached for Victoria.

But she wasn't there and that was what got him to open his eyes.

Bright sunshine flooded the room and hurt his eyes, but he worked through it, looking around the room for signs of her.

He had better plans for waking up this morning than to have to search for her. Unless, of course, she was in the shower and he could join her there.

With that in mind, he sat up in bed and swung his feet to the floor. The jeans he'd had on the night before were within reach and he yanked them on, standing to zip the zipper but not bothering with the button that fastened the waistband. He was hoping he'd have the opportunity to shed them again before too long.

He couldn't hear any sounds of water running as he descended the steps, though, and he didn't find Victoria in the living room or the kitchen when he got downstairs. The bathroom door was open, letting him know she definitely wasn't in there.

"Anybody home?" he called jokingly as he headed for the mudroom. But it, too, was empty and there was no answer to his question.

Maybe she was in his bedroom and hadn't heard him, he thought, picturing her propped on pillows in his bed, naked, waiting to surprise him with a change of venue for a little variety.

When he didn't find her in the bedroom, either, not only did his hopes of a morning of lovemaking fade away, he started to worry, to have doubts.

What if she'd taken off?

What if things between them the night before hadn't been as good as he'd thought they were and she'd gotten up this morning, snatched the keys to the truck and left?

With that thought Adam made a beeline for the front door, flinging it open to see if the truck was still parked out front. It was. But that wasn't what caught his attention.

Because there was Victoria, lying on the ground like a crumpled rag doll.

Calling her name, he charged from the cabin, ignoring the icy cold on his bare feet as he hurdled the porch and landed on the frozen ground.

She didn't budge. She didn't open her eyes. She didn't acknowledge him at all.

For a split second as he knelt beside her, he thought she was sleeping. That was how she looked, lying partly on her side, partly on her back, her arms and legs flung here and there.

Maybe she was a sleepwalker, he told himself. Maybe she'd walked out there in her sleep, laid down and gone right on sleeping.

But even as he had the thought, he knew it wasn't realistic.

Her skin was almost as white as the frost all around her and she was still. Too still.

"Victoria! Tori!" he shouted, hearing the panic in his own voice as it flashed through his mind that she was dead.

Nothing.

"Oh, God..."

And then he saw the faintest breath form a tiny cloud on the cold air near her nose and he knew she was alive.

Alive but hurt.

But as long as she was alive, there was hope, and that hope cleared his head.

He tried to assess the damage, gently checking her

arms and legs for broken bones. As he did he also noticed the ladder lying on the ground nearby and he suddenly knew what she'd been doing out there.

"That damn hammer," he muttered to himself, recalling that he'd seen it on the rooftop when they'd left the morning before for Whitehorn.

Why the hell had she gotten out of bed at dawn to climb onto the roof for a damn hammer?

But he knew why.

He knew it was his fault.

He knew that after a week of snide remarks and put-downs that when she'd either seen the hammer or remembered she'd left it there, she'd probably thought she'd better get it before he came down on her like a ton of bricks.

His fault.

It was his fault.

But he couldn't think about that now. He had to get help.

If they had been in town, he'd have called for an ambulance, but they were so far out that waiting for one to get all the way to the ranch didn't seem like a good idea. Not if he could get her into the truck and get her to the hospital himself.

He sprang to his feet then and ran inside the cabin, ripping the quilt and blankets from both his bed and the one upstairs that had been witness to so much pleasure the night before.

Then he grabbed a towel from the linen closet, too, threw on the first shirt his fingers touched in the closet and jammed his feet into his boots.

Back outside again he folded the towel and carefully immobilized her neck before covering her with the blankets. Then he raced to the barn, desperate to find anything he could use as a makeshift litter.

He spotted an old door discarded in one corner of the front stall and dragged it back to Victoria.

Hoping he wasn't doing anything that would cause any more damage, he very carefully eased her onto the door. Then he dragged it to the rear of the truck, lifted one end to brace against the tailgate, picked up the bottom portion and slid the makeshift stretcher and Victoria into the truck bed.

He secured the quilts and blankets around her, tucking them tightly beneath the old door to make sure she was as warm as he could make her.

She was still unconscious, but he saw her wince slightly and heard a small groan of pain as he jostled her.

"It'll be all right, Tori. I'll get you to the hospital," he told her, even though he didn't know if she could hear him or not.

He jumped out of the truck bed, closed the tailgate and dived behind the wheel to start the engine and pull away from the cabin with the gas pedal to the floor.

The whole time he was cursing himself for the stupidity of forcing Victoria to marry him, for dragging her out to the middle of nowhere, for doing all he'd done to her in the name of revenge.

And for possibly costing himself the best thing that had ever happened to him.

Nine

Adam was alone in the hospital's waiting room. It was just as well because he couldn't sit still. He could only pace, from one end of the area to the other and back again. Fast, frenzied, frantic.

The same way he'd driven into Whitehorn. The same way he'd spent the hour he'd been there, pausing only to demand news of Victoria every time he caught sight of someone. News that never came.

Still he paced, nearly out of his mind with worry.

Victoria had seemed to be regaining some consciousness when he'd pulled the truck into the emergency entrance with his horn blaring to gain attention. Doctors and nurses had rushed out to see what the commotion was, and within minutes they'd had Victoria on a gurney, rushing her into the hospital.

And leaving him to wait, not knowing what was going on, if she was okay. Leaving him to pace. To worry. To feel guilty.

Worry and guilt—they were like two demons nipping at his heels.

Worry and guilt made him chant over and over again in his mind, Please let her be okay. Please let her be okay....

Worry and guilt left him thinking that Victoria

might have been right when she'd compared him to Jordan Baxter.

Just considering that was a thorn in his side.

Maybe the reason it was such a thorn in his side was that it was true.

Not only was it true that he and Jordan had had similar hard-scrabble upbringings, that they'd both had to claw their ways to the top, Adam admitted to himself now, but what was Jordan Baxter doing in trying to block the sale of the Kincaid ranch to Kincaid heirs?

He was looking for retribution, that's what. He was hanging on to the past at all costs. He was trying to get what he considered his due.

Which is exactly what I've been doing.

Exactly.

Adam couldn't deny the comparison anymore. He'd been holding a grudge, just the way Jordan Baxter held a grudge against all Kincaids.

He'd been feuding with Victoria, with her family. Just the way Jordan Baxter feuded with the Kincaids.

No, he was no better.

"Damn it all to hell!" he said out loud just before a nurse came out from the examining rooms to write something on a clipboard behind the desk.

Adam made a beeline for the counter.

"Victoria Rutherford Benson," he snapped. "Do you know how she is yet?"

"I'm sorry. The doctor still hasn't reported any-thing to us."

Adam's fist hit the countertop all on its own and

he spun away from the woman, returning to his pacing, fast, frenzied, frantic.

Back came the thoughts of himself as just another Jordan Baxter.

It was not a comparison Adam liked and he jammed punishing hands through his hair in response.

It was not a comparison he liked particularly in regard to Victoria.

Things had not ended up the way they'd begun. Or the way he'd intended.

He hadn't factored in that he would come to care for her. That every breath he drew would seem worthy only if she was there. That the sun wouldn't seem to shine as brightly if she wasn't basking in it with him. That food wouldn't taste as good, or that flowers wouldn't smell as sweet, or that wind rustling through leaves wouldn't sound as peaceful, if he wasn't sharing it with her.

That life wouldn't be worth living without her.

And what had he done to the person who made him feel that way?

He'd abused her.

Okay, so not in the worst sense of the word. But he'd made her work like a hired hand and a maid. He'd been as contrary as a cobra. He'd forced her to marry him.

Even Baxter hadn't pulled anything that low and despicable.

Marry me or I'll make sure your parents don't have the money they need to keep your father alive…

That was about as low and despicable as it could get.

Suddenly all the years after that kiss in her father's barn—when he'd watched his own father sink farther and farther into a liquor bottle, when he'd watched his family disintegrate by slow increments, when he'd watched his mother struggle, when he'd struggled himself to help support them, to get through college, to make something of himself—all seemed less important.

Less important than what he'd done to Victoria since coming back to Whitehorn.

Less important than what he'd done to a person who seemed to be the reason his heart kept beating.

And now she was in this damn hospital, battered and maybe broken, and all because of him. Because of revenge and retribution and not being able to let go of the past.

Like Jordan Baxter.

And that was when Adam knew what he had to do.

If Victoria lived, he had to make this right. If Victoria lived—

That thought was unendurable so he pushed it away.

She had to live. That's all there was to it. She had to live and be well.

And he had to atone. He had to undo the damage he'd done. He had to make up for it in the only way he could—no matter how it hurt.

And it would hurt. It would rip him apart and he wasn't sure he would be the same afterward.

But he wasn't going to be another Jordan Baxter.

And being ripped apart to accomplish that was no more than he deserved.

When Adam stepped into Victoria's hospital room once the doctors finally allowed her visitors, the first thing she noticed was that he looked worse than she felt. And that was saying something because she felt pretty bad.

Her head throbbed worse than it ever had in her life and her whole body ached.

She'd been told she had a concussion and more bumps and bruises than anyone could count, but that the battery of tests and X rays that had been done on her revealed that nothing was broken, that there didn't seem to be any severe internal injuries and that she'd somehow managed to come out of the fall from the cabin roof without any life-threatening problems—probably because she'd had the good fortune to land on relatively soft earth.

The doctor had assured her that resting in the hospital today and tomorrow would make a big improvement. For the time being, the pain medication she'd been given made her as comfortable as possible, even if it did make her woozy.

But the truth was, just seeing Adam helped more than anything medical science could devise.

Even if he did look as if he'd been through the wringer.

"This was not how I planned for us to spend this morning," she joked weakly, forcing a smile she almost didn't have the strength for.

Adam kept standing with his back to the door, not coming nearer. And not saying anything. He merely studied her, solemnly, soberly, his handsome face lined and drawn.

Victoria felt chilled and she had the sinking feeling that he was mad at her again.

"I'm sorry about all this," she said then. "I know it was dumb of me to go up onto the roof when it was slippery, but it just didn't occur to me that it would be. I saw the hammer I'd left up there and wanted to get it down."

"Water under the bridge," he finally said, dismissing her explanation in a voice so low, so quiet, so serious, it was difficult to hear.

"Then I was going to sneak back into bed and wake you up," she informed him, trying for another weak smile and a hint of insinuation she hoped might coax him closer.

But nothing did the trick. He stayed where he was, staring at her.

Maybe she looked as bad as she felt, too, she thought.

She was about to say something along those lines when Adam's eyebrows pulled together and he said, "You scared the hell out of me."

She could hear in his voice just how shaken up he'd been and wondered if maybe that was what was wrong with him.

"They told me I'll be fine in a few days," she offered.

He nodded, as if he'd been informed of the same thing. But he still didn't leave his post at the door.

Victoria tried a different tack. She summoned every bit of strength and will she had and patted the mattress in invitation.

That only got her a darker frown when what she wanted was for him to sit on the side of the bed and hold her hand, kiss her and let her know everything really would be all right—because she was beginning to get the feeling that maybe everything *wouldn't* be all right.

"I've done some thinking while I was waiting out there for you," he said then.

Very formally, Victoria thought.

But even so, she didn't expect what he said next.

"I've decided to give you your freedom."

She really did feel light-headed and she wondered if she was actually hearing what she thought she was hearing. It seemed possible that she wasn't, that she was misunderstanding. How could they go from a night of passion to him breaking things off with her?

He was talking again and she forced herself to concentrate.

"I've already called my attorney and asked him to look into whether we need a divorce or an annulment. He'll also draw up the papers to file a quit claim deed on your parents' property. I'm giving it back to you free and clear to do with as you please. Keep it, sell it again, whatever. You can go back to

Boston, to your teaching, to your life, and forget this ever happened.''

So she hadn't misunderstood. He really was breaking things off with her.

Victoria felt as if she were hitting the ground all over again.

''What should I forget ever happened?'' she asked. ''The fall or the marriage?''

''Both,'' he said without having to consider it.

''I don't understand... What...'' All of the confusion she felt was there in her voice, raw and ragged. ''You're...ending things?''

''I'm giving you your freedom,'' he repeated as if nothing could be simpler.

It did sound as if it seemed simple to him. As if he were downsizing a company, laying off an employee the way he'd no doubt laid off many employees before.

But Victoria still couldn't believe her ears. ''So that's it? This is the end...of you and me? Of the marriage?''

''And of my going after any kind of revenge,'' he said as if confirming her list and adding to it. ''This was a mistake. I shouldn't have done it. I'm not even too sure what I was thinking to make you actually marry me. The past is the past and nothing can change it. I should have known that. I should have thought about it. But I didn't. I didn't think anything through until just now in the waiting room. So, yes, this is it. The end.''

Victoria felt very cold suddenly, despite the heavy

hospital blankets that covered her. "I've had my comeuppance and you've had your retribution, and now we go our separate ways—is that what you're telling me?"

"I'm just telling you that you're free."

"And last night...that was...what? Part of the plan? The culmination? The coup de grace?"

Even from the distance she saw him clench his jaw so firmly it flexed a muscle in his temple. "Last night was..."

But he didn't seem to know how to finish that.

"Last night was what?" she demanded, hearing her voice crack and wishing it hadn't.

He didn't answer her, though. He just shook his head and pushed himself away from the door to stand tall and straight and strong. But he still didn't take so much as a step in her direction.

"I'll have my lawyer contact you with the details," he said then. "If you need anything, just let him know."

"Mergers and acquisitions. Go in, take over, split things up, cast off the deadwood," she said, almost more to herself than to him, in a voice that echoed what she felt. "And I'm just the deadwood."

He started to shake his head again but stopped short, raised his chiseled chin slightly and said, "Have a nice life, Tori."

Then he turned and walked out.

No matter how hard she tried, Victoria couldn't help wondering if what Adam had put her through during the previous week was the punishment for her old crime, or if making her let down her guard and feel what she felt for him and then setting her free when it was the last thing she wanted had been his real goal all along.

But she did know one thing.

If she'd broken his heart twenty years ago, he had his restitution for it now.

Because he'd just done the same thing to her.

Ten

Never had Victoria spent a worse day and night than that following Adam's departure from her hospital room.

Pain—physical and emotional—was her only companion as she drifted into sleep, only to wake again and again with the sense that something was terribly wrong. Then she remembered that Adam had given her the heave-ho.

She sank into renewed despair that no amount of pain medication could ease before sleep overtook her once more to repeat the cycle.

Each time she recalled the cause of her emotional roller coaster, she asked herself if she could have been so blind that she hadn't realized that even in making love to her, Adam had only been seeking the best, most effective way to get even with her. As the hours wore on, she became more and more convinced that that was all his lovemaking had been about—misleading her so he could strike the final, most devastating blow.

By the middle of the next day she'd decided the best thing for her to do was to leave the hospital where she had nothing to do but marinate her own thoughts and dejection, and get out of Whitehorn as soon as she could.

A visit from her doctor after the lunch she sent back untouched gave her the go-ahead to be released. But just when she expected the next knock on the hospital door to be the nurse who was to go through her release instructions, Victoria was surprised to look up to find Crystal Cobbs poking her head into the room.

"Hi," Crystal said simply. "Want a little company?"

"Sure," Victoria answered, motioning the other woman in. "I'm just waiting for the papers I need to sign so I can be let go."

Crystal came into the room and sat in the visitor's chair, while Victoria raised the head of her bed so she was sitting straighter.

"I...heard you had an accident and were in here," Crystal said when they were both settled.

"There never were any secrets kept for long in Whitehorn," Victoria responded, assuming the town grapevine had somehow gotten hold of the information and spread it.

"What happened?" Crystal asked.

Victoria gave her the whole story.

Well, not the *whole* story, although there was a part of her that longed to confide in someone about everything that had happened. But she'd only just met Crystal and that didn't seem like something she should do to an almost-complete stranger. So she only explained the fall from the roof.

Crystal nodded through the entire tale as if she already knew most of it.

"So, how are you?" she asked when Victoria had finished.

Victoria couldn't answer that as fully as she would have liked to, either. She couldn't say that none of her physical injuries hurt as bad as what she'd felt since Adam had ended things between them. As bad as the fact that they had no future together. As bad as the fact that he wouldn't be a part of her life at all.

She had to stick to the health matters, briefly outlining them without going into too much detail.

Then Crystal said, "I, uh, also heard that Adam went back out to his ranch near the mountains rather than staying here with you. That seemed kind of odd. Is everything okay between the two of you?"

It was funny, but had that question come from anyone else it might have seemed like prying, like someone just looking for new grist for the mill. But from the first time Victoria had met Crystal she'd felt such a rapport with the other woman that that wasn't how Victoria took it.

She took it as genuinely concerned interest and she decided to suddenly give in to her need to talk to a friend, to give in to the urge she'd had to be completely honest and open, even if she didn't know the other woman well. And so she ended up pouring out her heart to Crystal Cobbs, hoping Crystal wouldn't mind too much.

"I knew something more was going on," Crystal said when Victoria had laid everything out, beginning with the teenage kiss in her father's barn and ending with how rotten she'd felt since seeing Adam for the last time.

"But you know what I think?" Crystal asked. "I think that things with Adam aren't what they seem."

"He made it pretty clear. He doesn't even want to see me or have contact with me. He said his lawyer would be in touch."

"Because seeing you would make it harder for him to go through with this. Harder for him not to be carried away by what he feels for you."

"What he feels for me is contempt."

"I don't think so. What I think is that he feels really, really bad that you were hurt in the middle of this revenge scheme of his and that turned everything around for him. I think he's fallen in love with you and can't stand that he brought harm to you in the process. And I'll tell you something else—I think you've fallen in love with him, too."

"Oh, I don't know about that," Victoria was quick to protest.

"Yes, you do. If you just let yourself recognize it. I also think that the two of you can have a happy future together if you can just open up to him, tell him you love him, and cross this one last hurdle."

Victoria wanted to believe that. She really did. But she was so afraid of even more rejection, of having to hear Adam tell her how much he really hated her, that not believing it was simply self-protective.

She shook her head in denial. "You don't know how cold he was. How—"

"I know from what you've said that he's a proud

man who has learned over time to detach himself from his emotions—maybe because he's known too much pain of his own from the years after that kiss. I know that if you don't go to him and tell him how you feel, you may never get together and you'll suffer for that your whole life."

Crystal sounded so certain.

Victoria could only wish she shared that certainty when in truth, she didn't.

It must have shown in her expression because Crystal said, "I'll tell you what. Let's check you out of here and I'll drive you to Adam's ranch. Just give honesty a chance and see what happens. If it doesn't work, all you have to do is call me and I'll come back to pick you up."

Face Adam again after he'd dumped her? Let him know how she felt? That seemed like asking for heartache and the proverbial slap in the face.

"What do you have to lose?" Crystal urged.

"My dignity, for one thing."

"Dignity won't keep you warm on a cold night. It won't keep you from pining for the man you love and wondering forever if it might have worked out between you if you had just had the courage to let him know how you feel."

"I didn't say I loved him," Victoria reminded her.

"Still," Crystal insisted. "Risking a little dignity in trade for a whole lifetime of happiness—that doesn't seem like such a bad deal."

That was true enough.

"All my things are still out there," Victoria mused, hearing the waffling in her resolve even before she knew she was actually considering Crystal's suggestion. "And I do need them one way or another."

"Perfect! An excuse to get you in the door." Crystal charged to her feet as if she were on a mission. "I'll go hurry up your discharge and pull my car up to the door. You get dressed."

Out Crystal went as if any delay might give Victoria the opportunity to change her mind. Which maybe she should do, Victoria thought even as she eased herself out of bed and gathered her clothes from the closet.

Maybe she should change her mind, accept that there was nothing between her and Adam but animosity and a bad past.

But something inside just wouldn't let her do that.

Something inside agreed with Crystal and told her she really had fallen in love with Adam. Long ago and again now.

Long ago, the love she'd felt for him had been puppy love, now it was more than that. It was a grown-up love. The kind she'd witnessed between her parents all her life. The kind that lasted. That kept two people together and sustained them through thick and thin.

The kind that couldn't be ignored.

Realizing that made Victoria finally understand why she'd been in so much misery since Adam had given her her freedom.

She didn't *want* her freedom.

She wanted Adam. And a life together and a family and everything they'd talked about, everything she'd ever dreamed of.

How was she going to have any chance for all that if she didn't go out to his ranch and tell him how she felt? If she didn't tell him that regardless of their bad past or their bad start now, he was the one man who could make her blood heat just by walking into a room. That he was the one man who could occupy her every waking thought and then still haunt her dreams. That he was the one man whose touch, whose kiss, she seemed to need more than she needed air to breathe. That he was the one man she could imagine herself spending the rest of her life with.

That he was the one man she loved in spite of everything.

And if he says, "Tough luck, I wasn't kidding. I don't want you"? she asked herself.

That thought stopped her in her tracks and made her reconsider everything she'd just talked herself into.

But then something else Crystal had said rang in her ears as if her newfound friend was there to repeat it.

Courage.

That was what Crystal had said, Victoria thought suddenly. That everything might work out if only she had the courage to let Adam know how she felt.

Victoria couldn't help reminding herself that courage—or the lack of it—was what had lost her Adam all those years ago.

The same lack of courage that could lose him all over again.

She couldn't let that happen. She might embarrass herself, she might sacrifice her dignity, but she couldn't let cowardice wreak any more havoc on her life.

So instead she went back to getting dressed and pointed out to herself as she did that even though Adam had ended the relationship he hadn't once said it was because he didn't want her. He hadn't once said he didn't care for her.

He'd said he'd made a mistake by forcing her to marry him. He'd said he hadn't thought it through. He'd basically said he hadn't realized what consequences it all might have had and now that he had, he was rectifying the situation.

Those weren't the same things as saying he didn't want her, that he didn't love her, she told herself to bolster that flagging courage. In fact, if he still hated her, wouldn't he have been satisfied with those negative consequences? Wouldn't rectifying the situation have been the last thing he'd have wanted?

And what about his actions?

Okay, so on the work front he'd been a little tough on her. But things had eased up—*he'd* eased up even before they'd made love.

She thought again about that night of lovemaking. It had been too incredible to have originated in anything less than a deep and abiding connection between them. Earlier he'd been too reticent to make love to her because he hadn't wanted it to be out of some sense of duty or obligation, out of any power plays or because she felt at his mercy. That wasn't the action of a man solely bent on revenge. It was more likely an indication that something else had been going on with him. That he could be as involved with her as she was with him.

Hadn't he told her himself how much the accident had scared him? Hadn't she heard it with her own two ears? Seen it with her own two eyes? Weren't those signs of the guilt Crystal had mentioned?

Victoria thought they were. He wouldn't have felt guilt if he still had only contempt for her. But guilt could have been the impetus for him to set her free.

"All ready to sign a few papers and hear my speech on how to take care of yourself so you can go home?"

The nurse's voice broke into Victoria's thoughts as the uniformed woman came into her room.

Victoria looked up from snapping the snaps on Adam's shirt—the shirt he'd worn the night they'd made love, the shirt she'd grabbed off the floor the next morning and had been wearing when she'd fallen, the shirt that still smelled of him. She knew she'd never be more ready than she was at that moment.

"Let's do it," she answered the nurse.

But she was talking about more than being released from the hospital. Because by then she'd worked up a full head of steam.

A full head of steam that she hoped would carry her right back into Adam's arms.

The hammer wasn't on the cabin roof anymore when Victoria arrived at Adam's ranch later that afternoon and she wasn't moving too swiftly as she got out of Crystal's car.

"Good luck!" Crystal said enthusiastically.

"Check your messages as soon as you get back. You may be making a return trip right away."

Crystal laughed as if she knew better, waved Victoria on, and called, "Look past the surface, that's my advice to you."

But even as Victoria headed for the house, she wasn't sure about the wisdom in this venture. Especially when the drive alone had taken so much out of her and left her with very little strength to face what she feared she was about to face. Merely walking up the porch steps was an exercise in agony that required her standing at the top of the porch for a moment before she could go any further. But, she decided, she'd come this far, she had to go through with it.

On the positive side, she thought, she already felt so bad maybe a rejection added to it would have less impact.

But she didn't actually believe it.

Once she reached the front door, she also didn't know whether to knock and wait to be invited in or to just go in unannounced.

It seemed odd to knock, but in the end that's what she did, opting for courtesy over surprise.

It felt like forever before the inside door opened. So long that Victoria began to wonder if Adam was out on horseback or in the barn.

Then there he was, standing on the other side of

the screen in nothing but a pair of jeans. His feet and glorious chest were bare and his hair was damp, as if he'd come straight from the shower.

The shock of seeing her registered on his face. "What the hell are you doing here?"

Not a greeting that encouraged her.

"Crystal brought me," she said dimly, wondering if she could flag down her new friend for a ride back to Whitehorn right then and there. But before she could do that Adam pushed open the screen door and scooped her up into his arms.

Apparently this time she really did look as bad as she felt, Victoria thought, assuming one glimpse of her was all it took for him to see how weak and worn out she was and to get her off her feet before she crumpled.

Inside, he set her gently on the couch, her back against one of the arms so her feet could be up on the seat cushions. Then he sat on the coffee table, facing her, and said, "You should still be in the hospital, not out gallivanting around. I don't know what those doctors were thinking to let you go or what you were thinking to come all the way out here."

Again, the chastisement was not encouraging.

"I needed to…" She almost told him the truth— that she needed to talk to him—but at the last second she changed her mind and instead said, "I needed to get my things."

"I could have sent them to you," he said, refuting her reasoning, all the while giving her a hard stare.

"And I wanted to give you back your shirt," she added as if that lent more weight to the errand.

His glance dropped momentarily to the shirt, to her breasts, before he seemed to force his eyes to her face again.

"Keep it," he clipped.

Victoria was feeling less and less sure about coming here. If Adam had anything but contempt for her it was hidden beneath the surface.

There she was, alone with him, without an immediate ride back to town and Crystal's urgings playing over and over in her mind.

What do you have to lose? What do you have to lose?

So goodbye, dignity, she thought, and plunged in.

"I wanted to talk to you, too," she finally admitted.

Adam frowned at her much the way he had the previous day, and even then he was so phenomenally handsome it nearly took her breath away.

But more than just being enamored of his good looks, she recognized her feelings for him welling up inside her and she knew all over again that she had to do this.

"Okay, well, I guess if making love to me was the crowning glory of your revenge, I'm going to give you the diamonds for that crown," she said more to herself than to him. Then she blurted, "I don't want my freedom."

His brows pulled so close together they almost became one.

But this time it was Victoria who rushed on before he could speak, mimicking Crystal's words to her.

"I'm in love with you and I think you're in love

with me and I want to work things out in this marriage and stick with it.''

That said, she felt as if she'd gone out onto the middle of a tightrope fastened with two frayed ends that could break at any moment.

Adam didn't put her at ease in any kind of hurry. He just went on staring at her, delving into her eyes with his.

Victoria was so afraid that he was trying to find the words to tell her that he wanted her out of his life forever that she didn't even draw a breath.

When he finally spoke it was in that quiet, solemn voice again. ''You're in love with me after all I did to you this past week?''

Slowly she let herself breathe again.

''A little hard work never hurt anyone.''

He looked at her pointedly. ''It hurt you.''

''Hard work didn't hurt me. Being dumb enough to get on a frosty roof hurt me.''

''I hurt you,'' he said so softly she barely heard him.

What she also heard was the undeniable evidence that he truly did feel guilty. Deeply guilty.

''Not as bad as I hurt you twenty years ago,'' she admitted the same way, all bluster gone and only the most sincere regret sounding in her tone.

For another long moment Adam held her eyes with his and Victoria wondered if he was thinking that too much hurt had passed between them for anything to conquer it.

But then she saw the lines in his face relax and the tiniest of smiles tempt the corners of his mouth.

"So you love me?" he asked.

Victoria had the impression that despite the light tone he used, he wasn't joking. And that now wasn't a time for her to joke back. That he needed to hear it as much as she did.

"Yes, I love you," she confirmed.

"Even after everything?"

"Even after everything."

"And you want to stay married to me?"

"Until the day I die," she said, hoping—praying—he wasn't making her bare her soul just to knock her down again.

But this was the risk she had to take, the last hurdle she had to cross, just the way Crystal had said. Now that she'd taken that risk and crossed that last hurdle, she was willing to do whatever she needed to do.

Adam didn't speak for what seemed like centuries, and Victoria felt suspended in midair on that frayed tightrope.

But then he closed his eyes and sighed as if an enormous weight had been lifted from his shoulders. When he opened his eyes again, he moved from the coffee table to sit beside her on the sofa, taking her hands in both of his.

"We're quite a pair, aren't we? We do our worst to each other and fall in love, anyway."

"Then you do love me?" she couldn't help asking on a gust of relief of her own.

Adam smiled at her, tenderly, sweetly. "I do love you. So damn much I didn't know how I was going to go on living without you."

"Then why set me free?" she demanded.

He chuckled a little. "I thought it was the least I could do after putting you in the hospital."

"*You* didn't put me in the hospital. I did that to myself."

"Because you were no doubt scared silly that I'd go ballistic over a forgotten hammer."

Okay, so he had her on that one. She wasn't even sure how he knew what she'd been doing up on that roof, but at that moment it didn't matter to her.

She was curious about whether or not she'd been right, though.

"Would you have gone ballistic over it?" she asked.

"No, I told you I put that bear into hibernation. And what was that stuff about my making love to you as the crowning glory of my revenge?"

Victoria shrugged—and winced at the pain the shrug caused her. "I couldn't be sure after you dumped me yesterday if that had been the plan all along—weaken my knees with lovemaking and then pull the rug out from under me."

He frowned at her again but this time it was only a mock frown. "I beg your pardon. What kind of a creep do you take me for?"

"No kind. Not anymore," she said easily, meaning it.

"I am a little peeved at one thing, though," he said then.

"What's that?"

"That now that we're going to have a real marriage I can't whisk you into bed to consummate it."

Victoria laughed. "No, I don't think I could live through that. Unfortunately."

"Maybe we could just whisk you into bed," he said, standing then to lift her into his arms once more.

He carried her into his bedroom and carefully set her on her feet.

"Clothes must be uncomfortable for you," he decreed, shedding his own pants to stand gloriously, magnificently naked before her.

Victoria feasted on the sight even as she laughed again. "My clothes didn't stop being uncomfortable for me by you taking your clothes off," she said as if he didn't know that and hadn't been teasing her.

Those words seemed to give him just the excuse he needed to bend over and remove her shoes, then slip her sweatpants down and unsnap the shirt in one fast tear, sliding the shirt off her shoulders and letting it fall to the floor with everything else.

He again swooped her up into his arms and laid her on his unmade bed where he joined her, pulling her oh-so-tenderly to lie naked body to naked body.

Victoria thought this was the best therapy because suddenly all her aches and pains eased. She snuggled against him.

He kissed her then. Finally! A deep, soul-searching, soul-uniting kiss that washed away every lingering doubt, every lingering fear, every lingering insecurity, and claimed her as his. This kiss was different somehow, more intimate, more open and uninhibited even though they both held passion at bay since she wasn't well enough to do more than that.

But that kiss, at that moment, in that way, was almost enough because nothing had ever felt as wonderful, as fulfilling, as satisfying, to Victoria.

Adam ended it and looked into her eyes once again, so intensely that she thought she could actually feel heat coming from them.

"I love you, Tori," he said as if he knew how much she was longing to hear it again.

"That was part of how I convinced myself to come here today," she confessed.

"You were that sure I loved you?" he teased.

She looked up into his chiseled, exquisitely handsome features and smiled a smug smile. "No. But you called me Tori yesterday, instead of Victoria." She parroted the stern way he'd used her name before. "It was like an endearment and when I remembered it, it seemed to soften all the harsh things you'd said."

"I gave myself away, huh?"

"Afraid so."

He gently hugged her closer. "Good thing."

Before too much time passed in their reunion Victoria felt the need to tell him one more thing.

"I'm going to make sure my parents know what really happened in the barn twenty years ago, that I was at fault for the whole thing. I know it won't make up for anything but—"

Adam stopped her words with another kiss.

Then he said, "It's all behind us. Yes, tell your folks so they won't hate their son-in-law, but then let's never talk about it again. Or about this past week, either. Let's just start over again from right here.''

Victoria smiled at him again. "I think I'd rather start from Saturday night. That was just too good to pretend it never happened.''

He smiled, too, with a hint of ego to it. "Liked that, did you?'' he asked, running a feather-light hand down her side and up to barely tease her breast and the nipple that had hardened all by itself.

"Didn't you?'' she challenged with a slight flex of her hips against his.

He groaned in a mixture of agony and ecstasy and flexed back. "Oh, yeah, I liked it all right. A whole lot.''

Then he kissed the top of her head and said, "But quit torturing me down there when you can't do anything about it.''

This time it was Victoria who groaned, wishing they could do something about it.

"Maybe if I have a little nap," she suggested.

"A little nap. A long nap. Whatever it takes,'' he answered her. "I can be patient when I know we'll have the rest of our lives.''

''Promise?''

"Cross my heart.''

Once more he kissed her, a blissfully sweet kiss, before he settled back onto the pillow and pressed her head to his chest to stroke her hair.

"Sleep," he ordered.

It wasn't a command Victoria could refuse because now that she honestly could rest, she really needed to.

And as she drifted into the first peaceful sleep she'd had since they'd made love Saturday night, she did it with the knowledge that this marriage would be more than one of convenience or retribution or comeuppance.

She knew it would be the real thing. Forever and ever. Until death did they part.

And that was the best bargain she'd ever struck.

MONTANA BRIDES
continues with

HONOURABLE INTENTIONS
by *Marilyn Pappano*

also on the shelves this month.
Turn the page for an exciting preview…

Honourable Intentions

by

Marilyn Pappano

Deputy Sloan Ravencrest sat at a red light, tapping out an intricate rhythm on the steering wheel and thinking about the drive he was about to take out to Winona Cobbs's Stop-n-Swap outside town.

There were some, including most of the other officers assigned to the Montgomery case, who would say he was wasting his time and the taxpayers' money. Winona Cobbs was a flake, a crazy old woman who talked with spirits and ghosts. She was forever coming forward with some bit of information gleaned from the "other side." She was crazy, but harmless.

On the other hand, there were some, including his father, his grandfather and most of the more traditional Cheyenne on the reservation, who accepted that "other side" as a natural part of life. They had visions, too, or knew people who did. They believed in mysteries and spirits and things logic couldn't explain. They didn't discount anything merely for lack of proof.

Sloan wasn't sure which group he belonged in. He had some faith, but he also had his share of skepticism. That was thanks, his father claimed, to his white mother. He had a foot in both the Cheyenne and the white worlds, so why shouldn't he straddle the line on this, too?

All he knew for a fact was that Winona had come by the sheriff's office a few weeks ago to recount her latest vision to him, one in which she'd claimed to see Christina Montgomery dead. And that neither the sheriff's office nor the police department nor the state bureau of investigation had any better leads to follow up. And that the powerful Montgomery family wanted answers yesterday.

And one other thing, he acknowledged with a grin as the light changed and he eased away from the intersection. He knew that Winona Cobbs's niece Crystal was just about the prettiest little thing he ever did see.

His grandfather, who'd helped raise him, would tell him he should be ashamed of himself, using his job to get an introduction to a pretty woman. But, hell, he'd tried every other way. He'd managed to bump into her on a couple of her rare trips to town, but she'd been in too big a hurry for small talk. He'd tried to get one of her few friends to coax her into the bar where a fair number of Whitehorn's single folks hung out, but that had been a no-go. He'd even done a little unnecessary shopping at the Stop-n-Swap, but she'd hardly looked at him.

His grandmother, who had also helped raise him, would tell him he was foolish, expending effort to meet a white woman. Hadn't it been a white woman who'd broken his father's heart? Who had abandoned Sloan on his father's doorstep three days after he was born to save her parents the shame of knowing they had a half Native American grandbaby? Why didn't he look closer to home? she would urge. Why not look for one of his own kind?

Because not one of his own kind had ever intrigued him the way Crystal Cobbs did. Maybe it was the way she looked—beautiful, with black hair, green eyes and pale china-doll skin. Fragile, with her defenses firmly in place whenever anyone came close.

Or maybe it was the way she talked—in a rich, lush Georgia drawl that put a man in mind of hot days, steamy nights and astounding women. Even curt brush-offs sounded incredibly sensual in her slow, honeyed voice.

Maybe it was the way she moved. Just last weekend he'd stood in the produce section at the grocery store and watched her select apples and tomatoes in a way that made his mouth go dry and his mind go blank. He couldn't have spoken to her to save his life, not after watching her long, slender fingers and their slow, enticing touches.

Maybe it was the look in her eyes when he did try to talk to her. Wary. Aloof. Distant. And, underneath all that, frightened. It was easy enough to guess that she'd been hurt. Why else would such an elegant Southern belle trade Georgia's gentility for Montana's rugged frontier?

It wasn't so easy to tamp down the protective feelings she roused in him. It wasn't at all easy when he watched her stroll through the market, touching this, damn near caressing that, to restrain the urge to wrap his arms around her and promise she would never be hurt again.

But he never made promises he couldn't keep. Since he hadn't yet managed to get beyond "Hi, how are you?" with her, the chances that he could protect her from anything were somewhere between slim and none.

Slowing down, he turned off the highway just outside of town into the dirt-and-gravel parking lot that fronted the Stop-n-Swap. In warm weather, Winona did much of her buying, selling and trading outside on a shaded patio, but the bulk of her goods were stashed in one giant room in a squat, concrete-block building. Much of it was junk, but if a person took the time to poke around, he could find some bargains. His grandmother's oak rocker had come from there, and half of Aunt Eula's Depression glass collection could be traced back there.

There was only one find Sloan was interested in. Maybe this third visit would be the charm....

* * * *

Don't forget

HONOURABLE INTENTIONS
is on the shelves now, and
THE COWBOY'S GIFT-WRAPPED BRIDE
will be available next month

MONTANA
BRIDES

0901/MB/RTLb